ANOTHER ME

ANOTHER ME

A NOVEL

EVA WISEMAN

TUNDRA BOOKS

Tundra Books, a division of Random House of Canada Limited,
a Penguin Random House Company

Library and Archives Canada Cataloguing in Publication

Wiseman, Eva, author
Another me / by Eva Wiseman.

Issued in print and electronic formats.
ISBN 978-1-77049-716-0 (bound).—ISBN 978-1-77049-718-4 (epub)

I. Title.

PS8595.I814A7 2016   jC813'.54   C2015-905460-5

C2015-905461-3

Published simultaneously in the United States of America by Tundra Books of
Northern New York, a division of Random House of Canada Limited,
a Penguin Random House Company

Library of Congress Control Number: 2015947647

Edited by Janice Weaver
Designed by Rachel Cooper
The text was set in Dante.
Printed and bound in U.S.A.

www.penguinrandomhouse.ca

1   2   3   4   5   20   19   18   17   16

Penguin
Random
House

TUNDRA BOOKS

For my parents
and for Nathan, Sam and Marni

There are more things in heaven and earth, Horatio,
than are dreamt of in your philosophy.

—William Shakespeare, *Hamlet*

PROLOGUE

The Angel of the Night is hovering over the city of Strasbourg as the boy makes his way home. It's so dark that he can barely see his feet as he scurries across the town square. His mind is full of her. He can still feel the silkiness of her hair beneath his fingers, still see the dimples quivering at the corners of her lips as she smiles. He can still hear her sweet voice soothing his spirits.

The cathedral bells break his reverie. He is so startled that he stops in his tracks, almost slipping on the icy cobblestones. Then he sees them on the other side of the plaza—three shadowy figures heading directly toward him. He hopes that they won't notice him. His clothes are dark and he pulls down the hood of his cloak to cover his face. Just then, the moon escapes the clouds and kisses the yellow badge on his chest.

He clamps his hand over it to make it disappear and wills himself to stand completely still, just another shadow in the vast square.

"Who's there?" cries a harsh voice.

"What's the matter with you, Anselm? You're seeing ghosts," says a voice full of ale. "You're afraid of your own shadow!"

"No, Anselm is right. I saw something moving too." The third speaker sounds older than the other two.

The boy breaks into a run. Feet come pounding over the cobblestones behind him. He sprints past the town well and shrinks down into the shadows cast by the cathedral beyond it. How he wishes for a knife in his grasp, but Jews are forbidden from carrying weapons.

He peeks around the side of the building. Three men are standing beside the well. They too are dressed in dark clothes. Two of them are bent under the weight of large sacks, while the third, a giant in the shadows, has a white cat squirming under his arm. The boy presses a hand over his mouth, for his breathing is so ragged and so loud that he's terrified they will hear him.

"There was somebody there," one of the men insists. "I would bet my last coin on it."

"Forget about it. Let's do what we came for," says his companion.

They turn to the well and empty their sacks into it. The boy's nose twitches from the stink of rotting food and feces. He hunkers closer to the wall of the cathedral.

"Did you hear a noise?" asks the man with the cat. He steps away from the well and moves even closer to the cathedral wall. The boy could touch him if he extended his arm. "Nothing here," he finally says.

"Let the Jews explain this!" shouts the man called Anselm. He sounds deep in his cups. He gestures to his cronies. "Your turn."

The giant raises the cat high into the air and throws it in the direction of the well. The animal misses its target and lands with a loud thud on the ground beside it. With a mighty yowl, it sets off into the darkness, barreling into the boy in the shadows. He jumps backwards, loses his balance on the slick cobblestones and ends up sprawled on the ground next to the animal. It rubs against his knees and begins to purr.

As he pulls himself up, he finds himself staring into a menacing face pushed close to his. His assailant is young, no more than his own seventeen years.

"Hey! Come over here and see what I've found," his attacker calls. He reeks of spirits.

His companions crowd around him. The first one, also his age, seems on the verge of collapse from drink. He grabs the cat and tosses it into the well.

There is yowling, a splash, a muffled thud. Then echoing silence.

"What have we here?" asks the one who found him. He points to the yellow badge on his cloak. "A Jew boy!"

"How fortunate," says the third man.

Now that the boy can see his face, he recognizes this person immediately. He could never forget that evil sneer crowning the red goatee.

"You again!" cackles the man. "You won't get away this time." He turns to his accomplices. "We'll leave the Jew by the well," he says. "We'll tell everybody that we came upon a bunch of them poisoning the well and tried to stop them, but there were too many. We'll say the rest of the Jews ran away, but we caught this one." He laughs and points at him. "We'll be heroes!"

"You'll never get away with it!" the boy cries. "I'll tell everybody that I saw you throw garbage and even the live cat into the well. Everyone will know that you poisoned the water and not my people!"

The man with the goatee gives a harsh laugh.

"You won't have the chance," he says as he lifts his knife high into the air. It glints coldly in the moonlight.

The blade descends . . .

NATAN'S STORY

CHAPTER 1

It all began three days ago, on the eve of our Sabbath. Shmuli and I were in the shed at the back of our house, folding the used clothing Papa had purchased. The neater the garments were folded, the more could be put into the wooden cart he used to take them to Drapers' Row.

"I'm tired," my little brother whined. He plopped down on a large pile of tunics, breeches and cloaks. "I don't want to work anymore."

"Shabbos is almost here. We'll rest then."

He stuck out his tongue but continued working, muttering complaints under his breath. I pretended not to hear. I was tired too, but our parents needed our help. Mama laundered the secondhand clothing Papa purchased. It was my job to sort the garments and fold them, and Shmuli usually helped me. Once he and

I had piled them into the cart, Papa harnessed himself
to it and pulled it down to Drapers' Row. We lacked
the money necessary to buy a mule for the job. Papa
trundled the cart from shop to shop, selling his fabric
to the drapers to turn them into luxurious garments
for their wealthy customers.

Our parents worked from early in the morning till
late at night—except on Friday evenings, when Mama
made us stop work early to bathe in the wooden tub
in the kitchen before the sunset. Once we'd passed her
rigorous inspection of the skin behind our ears and
of our hands, we changed into clean clothes to welcome
our Sabbath. Papa was never able to give her more than
a few coins to spend, but Mama always made sure that
our table was crowded with steaming pottage and suc-
culent pies and our Shabbos bread. Shmuli and I would
crowd around as she prayed over our Shabbos candles
and Papa said blessings over the bread and the wine.
Life seemed good and full of promise.

Just then, Shmuli brought me back to myself with
another complaint, and I glanced through the open
door at the sky. In a few minutes, we would have to
stop working. Mama appeared in the doorway. She
was wearing her best homespun gown, and a scarf of
many colors covered her hair. But a frown marred her
sweet expression.

Shmuli rushed up to her. "Mama, I don't want to—"

"Hush, Shmuli!" she snapped.

He fell silent, amazement written on his face. Mama was never impatient with him.

"I'm worried," she said, kneading her hands. "Your father isn't home yet and the sun has already begun to set. Your papa never comes home late on Shabbos."

"I'll go look for him," I offered.

"I'll come with you," Shmuli said.

"Don't wander too far," Mama warned us. "Two Jewish boys alone in the streets on the eve of Shabbos . . . it's asking for trouble."

I set off down Judenstrasse, the Street of the Jews, with Shmuli close on my heels. This close to the sunset, Judenstrasse was almost deserted, and I could see at a glance that Papa wasn't there. Shmuli and I crisscrossed the side streets but still could find no sign of him. We went all the way across the town square to Drapers' Row, but he was not to be found there either.

"Where could he be?" cried Shmuli, on the verge of tears.

"Let's look for him down the lane behind our house."

"Papa would never go that way," Shmuli said. "He told me it isn't safe there for Jews like us."

"We'll be quick. But we must check—it's the only place we haven't looked." I turned the corner, Shmuli following close behind.

"Look!" he cried.

A pair of legs splayed out at an odd angle from behind a mound of rubbish. A cart was upended beside them. I peered slowly around the trash, already knowing what I would see.

Papa's eyes were closed and blood covered his brow. Blood was also dripping from a deep cut on his temple. His face was ashen and his clothes were torn. Shmuli began to cry. This can't be happening, I kept telling myself. Please, Lord, let him be alive. I put my ear to his lips and felt his faint breath fan my face.

"Baruch Hashem, he's breathing!"

I tore a strip from the bottom of my cloak and wrapped it around his brow. With my brother's help, I lifted my father into the wooden cart and we hurried for home.

For three days Papa tossed and turned on his bed, full of feverish dreams. Not even the surgeon's bloodletting was of any help. I was glad that he remained senseless while the surgeon strapped one of his legs to a long wooden stick.

"His leg will heal in a few weeks if he rests it," the surgeon muttered in a gruff voice as Mama slipped a coin into his palm. "He is lucky only one of his legs is broken after the beating he received."

"Lucky?!" I blurted. "You call being beaten to within an inch of his life and left in the alleyway with the trash lucky?"

"Natan!" my mother hissed. Her face red with embarrassment, she turned to the surgeon and said, "Please forgive my son. He's young and he doesn't mean to be rude. Isn't that so, Natan?"

"Yes, Mama," I said grudgingly. "Forgive me. I'm only worried about my father."

The next morn, Papa regained his senses and awoke. He was weak but his brow was cool to Mama's touch. He insisted that I help him sit up on his pallet before he told us his tale. Mama helped him with a long draught of ale. Shmuli sat down beside him and snuggled close.

"What happened, Papa? Who did this terrible thing to you?" I asked.

He put down his tankard and began to speak. "I didn't want to be late for Shabbos, so I went down the lane to save time," he explained. "I didn't even see them coming at me until it was too late. There were three or four of them, I think. I can't be too sure, for everything happened so quickly."

He gestured to me to hand him the ale. He drank deeply before continuing with his story.

"'Filthy Jew!' they kept yelling. 'Give us the money you stole from your God-fearing neighbors!' I gave them the few coins in my purse, but that didn't stop them from beating me. I tried to fight back, but they had knives and I had no weapon. I didn't have a chance against them."

"Forget about them," Mama soothed. "You must rest and give your leg a chance to heal. That's all that matters."

"We need food on the table," Papa said. "I must go to Drapers' Row on Sunday to sell the garments I bought or we'll starve."

"That's out of the question!" Mama snapped. "You're not going anywhere in the state you're in."

He tried to stand up, but sweat broke out on his brow and he fell back onto his bed.

"My cursed leg," he moaned, wiping his brow with the back of his sleeve.

"I'll go to Drapers' Row in your stead, Papa."

"Absolutely not," he said. "It's not safe for Jewish boys on the streets of Strasbourg, no matter how much we pay for the protection of the city council. There's always somebody out there ready to insult us, to call us foul names. The members of the guilds hate us so much. I know how to handle them, but you're too young."

Papa had told me before about the guild members. These were men of the same profession who had joined together in a group to help each other and to establish rules for doing business. In Strasbourg there were guilds for butchers and cobblers and of course the drapers who were Papa's customers. But the guilds also existed to protect their own members—and especially to keep outsiders from setting up in trade—and Jews like us were among those excluded from those professions.

"There is no other way," Mama said reluctantly. "I don't like it any better than you do, but it'll take weeks for your leg to heal. We can't wait that long. We need money if we want to eat." I could see by her worried expression that she was trying to convince not only Papa but also herself. "The Lord will look after him."

I sat down on the bench beside my father and grasped his arm. "Let me help, Papa."

He smiled gently. "You're a good son, Natan—always ready to learn with your papa, always wanting to help me—but you have a temper. And that you cannot afford—not if you want to survive on the streets of Strasbourg. That's why I always refuse to take you with me while I try to sell my wares."

"I won't answer back, not even if people try to bait me. I'll ignore them, I promise."

He stared at me for a long moment, then nodded reluctantly. "We do need the money the clothing will fetch." He sighed heavily. "All right. You may go to

Drapers' Row, but only if I have your word that you'll be careful."

I put my hand over my heart. "You have it!"

"Take my cart, but go only to the shop of Wilhelm the draper. He is more honest with us than his colleagues in his guild. He sells bolts of material and some used clothing too. He's one of my best customers." Papa's voice was full of pride. "Wilhelm's shop is in the center of Drapers' Row. After you pass the cathedral, you will find him on the left side of the street. Tell him that you are Natan, son of Simon the Jew. Once he knows that, he'll treat you fairly."

"Can I go with Natan?" Shmuli asked.

"I don't know, Shmuli. A boy your age . . ."

Shmuli climbed to his feet. "I'm not a boy, Papa," he spluttered. "I'm eight years old."

Our father laughed. "All right, all right. You may go too, but only if you promise to listen to your brother."

Shmuli jumped up and down in delight. "We'll sell more clothes than you even dreamed of, Papa!" he cried.

CHAPTER 2

The stench of garbage filled the air as I pulled our laden cart down the gutter in the center of Drapers' Row. I was harnessed to the cart like an animal while Shmuli pushed on the back of it with all his might. We were wading through the filthy sludge in the gutter so we didn't have to shoulder through the masses of people surrounding us.

The dwellings on both sides of the street leaned toward each other like flowers leaning toward the sun; they almost met at the top, casting deep shadows into the lane. Only a sliver of sky peeking through indicated that the sun was up. As I passed the open windows of the shops, the drapers called out to me: "Come see my wares!" "Buy my merchandise!" and "We're the cheapest in Drapers' Row!"

My mission was to sell, though, not to buy. I kept my gaze fixed forward. Suddenly, there was a swishing sound above my head. As I peered up, somebody cried, "Look out below!" The contents of a slop bucket came pouring through the air toward my head. I jumped out of my harness and let the rudder of the cart fall to the ground. Luckily, only the pointed tips of my shoes were splashed. I bent down to dry them with my sleeve.

A shout from Shmuli made me straighten up.

"Stop him! Thief!" my brother cried.

"What's the matter?"

"A boy stole some clothing off the cart. He ran up behind me and grabbed some of the clothes before I could stop him."

"He couldn't have got far in this crowd. Which way did he go?"

Shmuli pointed down the left side of the street. "That way!"

I caught up with the thief in front of one of the drapers' windows. It was easy to identify him, for he had stuffed so many clothes under his smock that he looked like a woman with a babe in her belly. I grabbed him by the scruff of his neck, but he aimed a kick at my shin, loosening my hold. Before I knew it, he'd slipped out of my grasp and was gone. I was about to give chase again when a woman's voice stopped me.

"Oh, let him go! He's just a child."

I spun around to tell her to mind her business, but the words froze on my lips. Framed by the shop's open window like a painting was the most beautiful girl I had ever seen. A pale curl peeked out of her wimple and eyes as blue as the summer sky twinkled in amusement. I was suddenly aware of the coarseness of my robe and the hated yellow badge on my chest. I swept off my cap and bowed low with a flourish like I had seen knights on the streets do in front of their ladyloves.

"Your wish is my command, my lady," I mumbled in a voice that sounded false even to my own ears.

"I'm no lady," she laughed. "I'm Elena, the daughter of Wilhelm the draper."

"And I'm Natan, the son of Simon the Jew. I've business with your father."

"I'll call him for you." She stood up, the silk of her golden gown whispering as she rose.

"Don't leave me, mistress," I cried. "I want to talk to you!"

My audacity horrified me, but a demon seemed to have overtaken my lips. She sank back onto her stool and considered me earnestly.

"What do you want to tell me, Natan, son of Simon the Jew?"

A smile danced across her lips and my courage abandoned me. I became tongue-tied.

"Is this lout bothering you, Elena?" said a voice.

I turned around. A portly fellow in bright clothes, not much older than me, was standing in the street behind me. Strands of lank brown hair peeked from beneath his cap. His glare traveled to the yellow badge over my heart and stayed there.

"Nobody is bothering me, Hans," Elena said. "Natan here has some business with my father."

The boy gave me a hard look before going through the door leading from the street into the house. Elena gazed after him and shook her head.

"Hans is my father's journeyman," she said. I must have looked puzzled, for she added, "He works with my father, learning the draper's trade. He means well, but—"

She fell silent when the curtains over the doorway separating the shop from the rest of the house parted and an older man appeared. I knew immediately by the richness of his garments that he must be Wilhelm the master draper.

"What's going on here?" he asked.

I bowed deeply. "I am Natan, the son of Simon the Jew. My father has been ill. He asked me to bring his merchandise to you, sir."

Wilhelm sighed deeply. "Yes, I've heard of your father's troubles. I hope that his health is improving. He is an honest man. I hold him in deep esteem."

"Papa will be back to his old self before long. He asked me to tell you that he sent you the usual load of clothing. Unfortunately, a thief ran off with a few garments just now."

"Please don't worry," the master draper said. He reached into his pocket, pulled out a gold coin and pressed it into my palm. "Give this to your father with my wishes for his recovery," he said. "Elena will show you where to unload your cart."

It took me several trips to carry our wares from the cart to a storage room located behind the shop. Shmuli remained in the street guarding the empty cart. Had we left it alone for even a moment, it would have disappeared. The streets were full of thieves.

I helped Elena arrange the clothing on rough wooden shelves attached to the walls. Finally, the last breeches and tunics were put away.

Elena gave a sigh of relief. "We're finally done!"

I wiped the sweat from my brow with the edge of my cloak. "It's hot work."

"Then it's time for ale. Follow me!"

We left the house and made our way through a small garden behind it. She shooed away some chickens that were pecking at the dirt and blocking our way. She led me into a small building that stood in front of the wall that surrounded the yard. Inside, an old woman was stirring pottage in a cauldron over a fire. The smells coming from the pot made my stomach growl. The woman scowled in my direction.

"What are you doing, mistress, bringing one of his kind to *my* kitchen?" She stared pointedly at the badge on my cloak.

"Hush, Vera!" Elena said. "Natan brought new merchandise for Father and helped me pile it up in the storage room. He's thirsty. We must give him something to drink." She smiled at me sweetly and gestured at a bench beside a trestle table.

Before long, I was draining a tankard full of ale. She slid onto the bench opposite mine and took a long swallow from her own cup. I didn't know where to look. I peered at my hands, at the sooty ceiling, at the scrubbed table in front of me—everywhere but at her face. I wasn't used to talking to girls, especially one who wasn't of my own people.

Elena too kept her eyes modestly downcast. It was only by the tiniest smile tugging at the corner of her lips that I knew she was secretly laughing at me.

"So, Natan, the son of Simon the Jew, how is it that we've never met before? I know your father well. He does business with my father all the time."

"My papa is the one who sells our clothes. I sometimes help him purchase used clothing, but I mostly sort what he has bought." I put my tankard down. "I'd better go. My brother is waiting for me."

"Would you like to eat something before you leave? Vera's cooking is very tasty."

"Thank you, mistr—I mean, Elena." I corrected myself at her frown. "It's our custom to eat only our own food."

She looked puzzled but then gestured for me to wait. "Just a moment," she said. She filled a wooden cup with ale and handed it to me. "Give this to your brother." She lowered her eyes. "You can return the cup to me the next time you come by."

I couldn't get her out of my mind, even though we had only just met. Something about her had touched my heart. Was it the blue of her eyes, the gold of her hair or the music of her voice? I saw her face while I was sorting and folding garments for Papa's cart. Her smile swam before my eyes as I studied our holy books by the light of a candle. Instead of focusing on the commentaries of our sages, I began to scribble the following words on a piece of parchment:

Her eyes
Blue as the sky.
Her lips
Like poppies in the fields.
Her hair
Spun gold beneath my fingers.

Shmuli glanced up from his own studies. "What are you writing?" he asked.

I folded the parchment into a small square and slipped it into the purse I wore around my neck. It was growing dark outside. Mama and Papa had retired to their corner of the room and closed the curtains around their bed.

"Nothing of importance," I said. "Come, I'll help you."

He settled beside me, our Bible spread over his knees. He ran his fingers along the pages and tried to pronounce the Hebrew words. I corrected him when he needed it.

"Time for sleep!" Mama finally announced, her voice muffled by the curtains.

Shmuli groaned but rolled up his parchment and stripped off his doublet and breeches before crawling onto the pallet he shared with me. A few moments later he was snoring gently. I tossed and turned until Elena's smile finally lulled me to sleep. I saw it, once again, in my dreams.

CHAPTER 3

The following week my mother needed more yarn for a tapestry she was weaving. Mama was so skillful in bringing jousting knights and their ladyloves to life on her loom that Papa sold her tapestries to the households of nobles and master tradesmen. Of course, these transactions had to be made secretly, for Mama was both a woman and a Jew—strong enough reasons to exclude her from the weavers' guild.

"Your papa has already found a buyer for this tapestry, even before I'm done weaving it," she said with a satisfied smile. "It's almost finished, but I need a bit more scarlet yarn for my lady's gown." With her finger, she caressed the damsel riding her steed across the cloth, then shook her head regretfully. "I wish I had time to spin and dye my own yarn. That way, I'd get the exact color I want. I hope Wilhelm the draper will have the shade I need." She cut a strand from the spool of scarlet yarn in front of her. "Buy me two arm lengths, as close to this color as you can."

Just the excuse I was looking for to see Elena in the flesh once more!

Mama slipped a few coins into my hand. "Be careful! If anybody tries to draw you into an argument, don't answer them! Pretend that you don't hear them."

I slipped the money into the pouch around my neck. For an instant, my fingers tightened around the poem I had hidden there.

"I'll be fine, Mama. Don't worry about me." I drew the pouch closed, careful not to meet her eyes. "Do you still have the tankard from the draper's?"

"Oh, I'd forgotten about it!" She took it off a shelf and handed it to me. "Don't forget to thank him. It was so kind of him to remember your brother outside in the hot sun."

I didn't tell her that it wasn't Wilhelm but his daughter who had shown kindness to both Shmuli and me. I wanted to avoid the long tirade that was sure to follow if she found out I had spoken with a girl who wasn't of our faith. Apart from our business dealings with our Christian neighbors, Jews like us lived in a separate world.

— # —

At the sight of the large sign in front of Wilhelm's shop, my mouth dried up and my tongue thickened like Mama's pottage. Elena was inside the shop, at the window, helping an old woman make up her mind about a length of black material.

"It's too dear," the woman muttered as she fingered the cloth with her gnarled fingers. Her expression confirmed her regret. "I wish I had the money for it. My daughter wants me to look nice at her betrothal."

"What if I reduce the price, Mother?" Elena asked with a smile.

The woman broke into a toothless grin. "Thank thee, mistress. That would suit me just fine!"

When the woman left, Elena turned to me. "So what brings you here, stranger?"

I handed her the yarn. "My mama needs yarn this color, two arm lengths."

She walked to a shelf at the back of the shop and held up the strand against two gigantic spools of crimson thread. She cut a finger's length from each spool and brought the samples over to me.

"Which color do you prefer?"

I stared hard at them, but they seemed the same to me. "I don't know . . ."

She took pity on me and pushed one of the samples into my palm. "Take this one. The color is a close match to your mother's yarn."

"Thank you. Please cut me two lengths." As I fumbled with my coin purse, I noticed the wooden tankard I had put on the counter. "Oh, I also want to return your tankard. Thank you for being so kind."

Her cheeks turned rosy. "Don't be daft, Natan. It was just ale." As she handed me the yarn I needed, she kept her eyes fixed on the merchandise.

I became emboldened. "I was happy to have an excuse to come to your shop," I said. "I wanted to see you again."

"I thought you had forgotten me," she whispered.

I could feel the heat rising in my cheeks. "Never, mistress! Never! I didn't know if you would want to . . ."

My fingers went to my coin pouch and the poem it held, but I didn't dare give it to her. She stepped closer.

"I wanted to see you again," she whispered.

Thank thee, Lord, I said to myself. I smiled at her with more confidence than I felt, and my hand moved toward the pouch around my neck once more.

"Then, I would like to—"

"Elena, your father wants to talk to you."

A harsh voice interrupted my words. My hand dropped. Hans, Wilhelm's journeyman, came into the shop through a door at the back. An angry frown distorted his sallow face. He took a few steps toward Elena.

"Is the Jew bothering you?"

"Don't be foolish, Hans," she cried. "And mind your manners! Natan is here to buy yarn for his mother."

She turned her back on the lout and locked eyes with me as she bent down to pick up the tankard.

"I'll meet you in the lane tonight," she whispered. "Behind the wall at the back of our garden. Be there when the cathedral bells strike eleven times. Knock on the wall when you get there."

I could barely untangle my thoughts from the hammering of my heart as I hurried toward our house in Judenstrasse. She wants to see me! She wants to see me! I crowed to myself. But then harsh reality intruded. Jews were not permitted in the streets of Strasbourg after eight o'clock in the evening. If I was caught leaving my house after curfew, I would be severely punished. But then I remembered the sweetness of Elena's smile and the softness of her voice, and I told myself I would find a way!

I lay as still as I could, listening to Shmuli's even breathing before gingerly sitting up, making as little noise as possible. I listened carefully. Papa was snoring loudly behind the curtained-off sleeping quarters he shared with Mama. The whole house was sleeping.

The fire was dead in the fireplace and the room had an October chill. I pulled on my breeches and wrapped myself in a cloak before tiptoeing out the door. Fortunately, Judenstrasse was very dark. Only a few stars lit my way as I headed toward the end of our street. I was careful to press myself against the houses lining the road, becoming just another moving shadow. Good fortune was on my side. I didn't meet the night watch.

Before long, I was tapping on the wall that ran along the back of Elena's garden. A gate, well hidden by a bush, creaked open and she appeared. Her face, framed by her white wimple, betrayed her anxiety, but her expression softened when she saw me.

"I was afraid that you wouldn't come, that you thought I was too bold," she whispered, her gaze fixed on the ground. "I don't want you to think I have ever asked another boy to meet me. My own boldness horrifies me."

Her distress gave me the courage I needed and I grasped her hand. "Dear mistress, never would I think that. Nor would I want you to believe it is my habit to visit maidens in the darkness of the night. I'm full of admiration for you. It fills my heart with joy that you found me worthy of your notice."

She smiled gently and pulled her hand out of mine. "Come with me," she said.

She led me back into the kitchen where she had given me ale a few short days ago. We sat down in the same spot where we had sat before. I gathered my courage once more and handed her the poem I had written for her.

"I have no jewels to give you, Elena. Only my poor words can express my regard for you."

She unfolded the parchment and handed it to me.

"Read it to me."

"No need," I said. "I know the words by heart."

I told them to her.

"So beautiful," she said. "You have the heart of a minstrel. I've never met anybody like you."

"Nor have I met anyone like you—so gentle yet so brave."

She turned her head away, but I could see in the starlight sneaking through the high window that she was smiling. Then we began to talk. And we talked and talked and talked until the sun peeked over the horizon and I had to bid her farewell.

"Return to me, my minstrel," she said as I bade her good-bye.

My brother and my parents were still asleep when I returned home, but Shmuli woke up for a moment when I lay down beside him.

"Where were you?" he asked, rubbing his eyes,

"The privy."

He was asleep again before I even finished speaking.

From that night on, Elena and I met several times every week, and she became the anchor of all my dreams. Before long, I couldn't imagine life without her sweet presence.

CHAPTER 4

NOVEMBER 1348

E lena told me that it was her duty to fetch water for her family. She went to the town well every day when the sun reached the top of the sky. I was determined to meet her there because I wanted to see her beautiful face in the sunlight.

I dressed in my warmest cloak, for winter was in the air. Mama was pleased when I offered to get our water.

"Be careful who you talk to," she warned. "Your father told me that a traveling merchant brought Rabbi Weltner a letter from his brother, who lives in Bern. The letter says that the sickness has arrived in that city." She sighed deeply. "More and more people are dying there every day. The Jews of Bern have been accused of poisoning the wells of the town to bring on the sickness. Several of them were arrested and tortured on the wheel until they confessed to the crime. Then they were put to death." She drew a worried hand across her brow. "Who wouldn't confess if they were tortured? Rabbi Weltner's brother wrote to warn him that the same kind of thing could happen to us in Strasbourg."

"Oh, Mama, it's so unfair! It shows how much they hate us."

She kissed me on the cheek. "That's why you must be careful," she repeated. "I couldn't bear it if anything happened to you."

"I won't do anything rash. I promise."

Guilt squeezed my heart with all its might, and suddenly I wanted to tell her about Elena more than anything in the world. But I allowed my words to die on my lips, for I knew Mama well enough to realize that she would be upset. She'd point out that both Elena and I were breaking the law prohibiting Jews and Christians from fraternizing. She'd warn me that we'd be put into the stockades if the authorities discovered our relationship. She would be so frightened that she'd surely forbid me ever to see Elena again. I didn't want to risk that, so I picked up the buckets and set out for the town square without saying another word.

I couldn't see Elena anywhere. Instead of the usual organized chaos in the square, all the merchants, artisans, knights and ladies were gathered by the well, pushing and shoving each other.

"Show the damned Jew that he can't get away with it!" cried a man in the middle of the crowd.

"Make him pay!" said another. "He surely makes us pay enough. This'll teach him to stop demanding the settlement of his cursed loans."

"Let's see how high and mighty the Jew acts now," cackled a woman behind me.

I shouldered my way to the front of the mob. Lying on the cobblestones was old Meyer, a moneylender who lived two doors away from us. One man was tugging and pulling on his snowy beard, while another was kicking him. A third—an absolute giant—was pouring water from a jug into the old man's mouth, making him cough and sputter.

"Let's see how you like drinking the water you poisoned, you bloody Jew!" the giant hissed.

Violent choking noises were the old man's sole reply. The other people in the crowd were laughing, clapping, encouraging the attackers.

"Kaspar, I beg you to think of what you're doing. He may be a Jew, but he's a man too."

It took me a moment to place the lone voice of dissent. But then I turned and saw Hans, Wilhelm the draper's journeyman. He was wringing his hands and was white with fear. I ran to him.

"Go and get your master!" I ordered. "Be as quick as you can!"

He scowled. "You can't tell me what—"

I pointed at the giant in front of us. "He'll kill the old man. Get Master Wilhelm, now!"

He turned on his heel and ran. I grabbed the man with the jug and spun him around by the arm, pulling him away from the moneylender. I was confronted by an angry face with a red goatee.

"What do we have here? Another cursed Jew!"

He grabbed me by my tunic and lifted me into the air before throwing me to the ground and pummeling me. I covered my face with my hands to protect myself, peeking through my fingers at the scene above. A large boot suddenly obscured my vision of the sky. Then pain in my head and all was blackness.

Shadows filled the chamber when I awoke. My eyes traveled around a grand room I had never seen before. Mama was sitting on one side of my bed, Elena on the other. I must be dreaming, I told myself. But I didn't want the dream to end, so I closed my eyes again.

"He is awake!" Elena cried.

Mama leaned over me and patted my face with roughened fingers. "Are you finally with us again, my son?"

"Where am I?" My eyes rested on a huge fireplace, on carved furniture and on walls hung with tapestries.

"You're in my home," Elena said.

I tried to speak, but my mouth was so parched that no sound came out. Mama held a cup to my lips. The ale tasted bitter.

"You had us worried," she said. "We were about to send for the surgeon to apply leeches to you." She laughed at my disgusted expression. "Elena's father saved your life, just as you saved the life of Meyer the moneylender." She wiped away a tear. "That was a brave thing you did. Brave but unwise."

I tried to sit up, but pain exploded in my head. I lifted my hand and explored the thick bandage wound around my temple.

"What happened?"

"It was gallant of you to defend the old man," Elena said.

"Brave but foolish," Mama repeated in a severe voice. "First your father and now you . . . What next?"

"What happened to the moneylender?"

"When his attackers turned on you, he crawled away into the crowd," Elena said. "Nobody was paying attention to him. Everybody was watching you. The old man somehow made his way home."

"He is resting in his bed," Mama said. "His wife was here a short while ago to ask about your health. She says that her husband will recover." She bent over me and straightened my covering. "Do you want more ale?"

I shook my head gently. "Why am I here?"

"Hans ran to get my father when you were attacked."

"As soon as Master Wilhelm appeared, Kaspar the butcher ran away," Mama explained. "He is a devil but too cowardly to tangle with a man as respected as Wilhelm the draper."

"My father had you carried to our house," Elena added. "He said it would be safer for you to heal here than in your own home. Nobody would dare to bother you here." She bent over me to straighten my blanket. "The inhabitants of our city hate your people so much. I just don't understand why."

"They hate us because we are moneylenders and men of commerce. They forget that these are the only professions open to us—that all other trades are forbidden to us," I explained. "They don't know that the city government takes most of our profits away. We must charge high interest in order to pay the taxes that have been imposed upon us in return for protection by the city."

"Enough talk! You must rest!" Mama said. "We can never repay Master Wilhelm's kindness," she added, her voice thick with emotion.

She stood up and marched to the doorway with Elena in her footsteps. But just before she followed my mother out of the room, my beloved locked eyes with me and gave a little smile. I hugged that smile to my heart as I fell into a deep and dreamless sleep.

I began to feel like myself as the days passed. My bruises faded from black and blue to an interesting shade of amber. And although my heart was filled with joy whenever I saw Elena, I missed my family. I decided to tell her father that I wanted to go home.

I was on my way to find him when I heard voices drifting out of a small chamber down the hall from the room where I was staying. I couldn't hear what was being said, but I could tell that a man and a woman were talking to each other. I thought it must be Wilhelm and Elena, and I decided this was my chance to thank the master draper for saving my life and to tell him that I wanted to return to my family. I also wanted to offer him my services in repayment for his kindness.

As I approached the chamber, I noticed that the curtain over the doorway was partially open. I stopped for a moment to compose my thoughts. I could see into the room. There were two people there. Elena was sitting in a high-backed chair, but it was Hans she was with, not her father. He was kneeling in front of her, his face flushed crimson, one of her hands held to his lips. Neither of them noticed me.

I took a step back so I could still look into the chamber without its occupants seeing me.

"Have you taken leave of your senses, Hans?" Elena was saying. She tried to pull her hand away, but he wouldn't let go.

"Nothing would make me happier than if you agreed to become my wife, Elena," he pleaded. "Please say that you'll marry me!"

I was about to dash into the chamber to thrash him, but the sincerity in his voice gave me pause. And would Elena want me to interrupt them? I stood there, undecided about what to do.

"I cannot marry you, Hans," Elena said.

"Why not? I'll be a master draper one day, just like your father. You'll never want for anything if you become my bride."

"Oh, Hans," she said, her voice softening. "I don't care about that."

"Then why won't you marry me?"

His voice was plaintive and he seemed on the verge of tears. Elena looked at him for a long moment, choosing her words carefully.

"I can never be your wife. I'm sorry, but my heart belongs to another."

My own heart soared.

Hans dropped her hand and stood up with effort.

"It's that Jew, isn't it? He's turned your head with his

handsome face, his curly hair and his tall carriage!" he cried. "You won't marry me because of him!"

"Natan has a name," she responded coolly, rising from the chair. "And why do you dislike him so? He has never done you any harm. Is it because his people are of the Jewish faith?"

Hans pulled himself up straight. There was an unexpected dignity about him that I had never noticed before.

"You do me a disservice, madam," he said. "I don't care how the Jew worships his God. I hate him because you chose him over me!"

"I chose no one," Elena replied in a cold voice, pulling open the curtain at the doorway. I rounded the corner just in time to avoid colliding with her.

"Shh!" I put my finger to her lips. "He'll be gone in a moment."

We waited until Hans left the chamber. He turned the other way and didn't see us. As soon as he was gone, I led her back into the room.

"I heard his proposal," I told her. "I'm sorry. I know I shouldn't have listened, but I couldn't help myself."

"Hans is full of conceit, but his intentions are good. He meant to honor me."

"Yes, he would look upon bestowing his name on you as an honor. I found the part where he imprisoned your hand most interesting."

"If you just knew how sweaty his palms are!" She wrinkled her nose in distaste. "His fingers are so stubby, and there is hair growing on their backs."

I couldn't help glancing down with satisfaction at my own long, lean fingers.

"I also found it fascinating that you told him your heart belongs to another." I looked at her innocently. "Tell me, my lady, who does it belong to?"

She danced away from me, giggling. "I'll let you guess that for yourself, my lord!"

Then she ran out of the chamber so quickly that I couldn't catch her.

I dreamt of her that night. I was in the town square, and suddenly, there she was, walking toward me. I opened my arms wide.

"Elena, come to me!"

She looked at me but hesitated, then broke into a run in the opposite direction, away from me.

"Where are you going? It's me, your Natan!"

She didn't stop.

When I finally awoke, there were tears in my eyes.

CHAPTER 5

As we left the synagogue, Papa was debating Rabbi Weltner's Torah lesson with our fellow congregants and Shmuli was running around in the snowy street with his friends, so neither of them noticed when a very dirty urchin bumped against me.

"Hey, watch where you're going!" I cried.

Something was pressed into my palm, and then he was gone. I opened my fingers to find a tiny piece of rolled-up parchment. I knew that only one person would be sending me notes. It had to be Elena. I tightened my fingers around it without showing it to anybody.

The smell of cholent greeted us as we arrived home, making my mouth water.

"Lunch will be ready in a few moments," Mama said. "Before we eat, Natan, could you please pick some herbs for me in the garden?"

In addition to weaving beautiful tapestries, helping Papa with his cloth trade and taking care of our family, Mama was also well versed in the healing arts. She grew herbs and other medicinal plants in a small patch of green at the back of our house. Some of the herbs were so hardy that they sprouted through the snow. Mama ground them up, boiled them and mixed them with secret ingredients to turn them into potions and poultices for members of our community. She was respected far and wide as a healer.

I told her that I would get the herbs and hurried to the garden. I made sure that nobody was around before I unrolled the parchment. It was short and to the point:

Must meet you tonight!
The usual place when the clock strikes twelve.
Yours,
E

This was the first time Elena had written to me. What could have happened that she had to see me so urgently?

I knew it wouldn't be easy to leave our house at midnight. The hatred against us had increased with the growing rumors that Jews were responsible for the plague. In response, our city government had sent armed sentries to guard both ends of Judenstrasse.

We were told that this was done for our own protection, but the sentries didn't allow anybody to leave the street after curfew.

In spite of the risks, I was determined to go. If Elena needed me, there was no other choice. I knew I wouldn't be able to figure out a way to elude the sentries, so I hoped that I'd be lucky and not meet them.

I waited until my family was asleep before I wrapped myself in my warmest cloak against the bitter cold and slipped out of our home, quiet as a mouse. I was careful to press myself into the shadows as I made my ghostly way through the darkness. I didn't come across the night watchman, but as I approached the end of the street, I heard voices. I stopped, melting into the building behind me. There were two sentries leaning against the wall of the house on the corner, across from the half-open gate that marked the street of the Jews. I stood there listening to them, my heart beating so loudly that I was amazed they couldn't hear it. The men were drinking, laughing, clinking their cups of ale. The curved blades by their sides glistened in the darkness.

The cathedral bell rang twelve times. I was late. Elena would think I wasn't coming, but I had to bide my time until the sentries were ready to leave. It seemed like hours but it must have been mere minutes until the taller sentry put away his cup.

"Time for our rounds," he said to his companion. "You go left and I'll go right."

The second man wiped his mouth with the back of his hand. "All right, all right. But I don't know why you care so much what happens to these damned Jews."

The first sentry snorted. "I couldn't care less what happens to them! The sooner they depart to hell, the better I'll like it. What I do care about is the money the Ammeister is paying us to guard them. So let's go!"

As soon as they left, I went through the gate and broke into a run for Elena's house. She was waiting for me, her pale, anxious face barely visible in the darkness. She drew me into the kitchen building.

"I was afraid you wouldn't come," she whispered.

I touched her shoulder. "Nothing will keep me from you. Not all the sentries in the city. But what's wrong? Why did you send for me?"

"I overheard my father talking to the Ammeister, Peter Schwarber. He told Papa that an assembly was held in the Alsace region. There were delegates there from the cities of Bern and Zofingen, and they claimed that the Jews in their towns had poisoned the wells, causing an outbreak of the Black Death. They said that these Jews confessed to this crime under torture."

I nodded. "Yes, Mama told me that our rabbi received a letter about this same terrible situation.

No wonder those poor Jews confessed. Wouldn't you confess to anything if you were tortured?"

"Anybody would! I'm only telling you what I overheard. Schwarber also told my father that these delegates convinced the representatives from the cities of Basel and Freiburg to join them in killing all the Jews in their own communities." She grasped my arm. "They asked the Ammeister and the other Strasbourg envoys to do the same," she whispered.

"What did Schwarber say?"

"He refused. He said that the Jews of Strasbourg pay dearly for letters of protection from the city. He also said that the Jews pay higher taxes than any other citizens, and that they are important to the wealth of Strasbourg. He refused to harm the Jews in our city."

I took both her hands in mine. "Why are you so worried, then? The Ammeister stood up for us. He'll protect us."

"He did, but he also told my papa that he will order the well in the town square covered so that nobody will be able to use it. Why is he planning on such an action if he is so certain of your innocence?" She stepped so close that her breath fanned my face. "How long can he keep you safe? I'm so frightened! You and your family must leave Strasbourg. It's dangerous for you to remain here."

"We have nowhere else to go."

"I will pray every night that you find a safe place."
Her face was drained of color.

I pulled her into my arms. "You worry too much."
I smoothed away the furrow between her brows until
she gave the ghost of a smile. Then I kissed her and told
her I loved her. She told me she loved me back. We were
alone in the world. Nothing else mattered—not my
parents' anger if they found out about us, and not the
punishment of the law that forbade us to be together. I
kissed her again and drew her so close that I could feel
her heart beating.

She pushed me away. "I can't," she whispered.
"I want to, but we mustn't."

"But, Elena—"

She backed even farther away from me.

"Tell me a poem. I love to hear you talk."

So I repeated to her the words my mother sang to
me every night when she settled me into bed when I
was but a babe:

> The stars are the souls
> Of loved ones
> Gone, never to return.
> Never to meet us again
> Until the end arrives.

The stars look down upon us
And keep us safe
From danger and need.
Their love is a cloud of protection
We feel but cannot see.

She laid her head on my shoulder.

"So beautiful," she whispered. "Nobody else I know has words like you." She snuggled against me. "Please be careful. I'd be lost without you."

Her concern imprisoned my heart. I swore to myself never to disappoint her. We talked and the hours passed and we didn't even notice. She began to weep when I said that it was time for me to leave her.

"Don't cry! I have to go home before my parents awake."

"I suddenly feel as if I'll never see you again," she said.

"I'll come again tomorrow at the same time."

"But if the sentries catch you . . ."

I stroked her cheek. "Don't worry. I'll be here. Nothing can keep us apart."

Then I left her.

CHAPTER 6

The Angel of the Night was hovering over Strasbourg as I made my way home. It was so dark that I could barely see my feet as I scurried across the town square. My mind was full of her. I could still feel the silkiness of her hair beneath my fingers, still see the dimples quivering at the corners of her lips as she smiled. I could still hear her sweet voice soothing my spirits.

The cathedral bells broke my reverie. I was so startled that I stopped in my tracks, almost slipping on the icy cobblestones. Then I saw them on the other side of the plaza—three shadowy figures heading directly toward me. I hoped that they wouldn't notice me. My clothes were dark and I pulled down the hood of my cloak to cover my face. Just then, the moon escaped the clouds and kissed the yellow badge on my chest. I clamped my hand over it to make it disappear and willed myself to stand completely still, just another shadow in the vast square.

"Who's there?" cried a harsh voice.

"What's the matter with you, Anselm? You're seeing ghosts," said a voice full of ale. "You're afraid of your own shadow!"

I broke into a run. Feet came pounding over the cobblestones behind me. I sprinted past the town well and shrank down into the shadows cast by the cathedral beyond it. How I wished for a knife in my grasp, but Jews were forbidden from carrying weapons.

I peeked around the side of the building. Three men were standing beside the well. They too were dressed in dark clothes. Two of them were bent under the weight of large sacks, while the third, a giant in the shadows, had a white cat squirming under his arm. I pressed a hand over my mouth, for my breathing was so ragged and so loud that I was terrified they would hear me.

"There was somebody there," one of the men insisted. "I would bet my last coin on it."

"Forget about it. Let's do what we came for," said his companion.

They turned to the well and emptied their sacks into it. My nose twitched from the stink.

"Let the Jews explain this!" shouted the man called Anselm. He sounded deep in his cups. "Your turn," he said to the third man.

The giant raised the cat high into the air and threw it in the direction of the well. The animal missed its target and landed with a loud thud on the ground beside it. With a mighty yowl, it set off into the darkness, barreling into me in the shadows. I jumped backwards, lost my balance on the slick cobblestones and ended up sprawled on the ground.

As I pulled myself up, I found myself staring into a menacing face pushed close to mine.

"What have we here?" the fellow slurred. He pointed to the yellow badge on my cloak. "A Jew boy!"

"How fortunate," said the third man.

Now that I could see his face, I knew him right away. It was Kaspar! I could never forget that evil sneer crowning the red goatee.

"You again!" he cackled. "You won't get away this time." He turned to his accomplices. "We'll leave the Jew by the well," he said. "We'll tell everybody that we came upon a bunch of them poisoning the well and tried to stop them, but there were too many. We'll say the rest of them ran away, but we caught this one." He laughed and pointed at me. "We'll be heroes!"

"You'll never get away with it!" I cried. "I'll tell everybody that I saw you throw garbage and even the live cat into the well. Everyone will know that you poisoned the water and not my people!"

Kaspar gave a harsh laugh.

"You won't have the chance," he said as he lifted his knife high into the air. It glinted coldly in the moonlight as it descended.

Then pain and darkness, and finally . . . oblivion.

"Good riddance," Kaspar said, kicking my body on the ground. He pressed his knife into my palm and closed my fingers around the handle. "Anselm," he barked at his friend, "go for the night watch. I'll stay here with Bertrand to guard the dead Jew." He snickered. "We'll tell the watchman our story when you bring him back with you."

Anselm obeyed without hesitation. Kaspar and Bertrand remained by the well. They jumped up and down and rubbed their hands together to stave off the bitter cold.

I stood beside them, looking down at myself. I—Natan, son of Simon the Jew—looked so peaceful on the icy cobblestones. I was lying on my side, my eyes tightly shut. The knife that had killed me was clutched in my hand. I hunkered down, bending over my own body in the darkened square, and traced the outline of the round badge of the Jews on my cloak.

I could see that the yellow cloth had been stained bright crimson.

Just then, footsteps shattered the silence. Hans appeared, staggering and singing:

My true love was lost to me,
Forever and forever gone from me.
My true love was lost to me,
Forever and forever gone from me.

He stumbled over and dropped to his knees at my side.

"What have we here?" he asked, leaning over me. "It cannot be! It cannot be!" he cried.

"Get away from the Jew!" Kaspar roared.

"Kaspar, may God forgive you, what have you done?" Hans cried.

He struggled unsteadily to his feet. He turned as if to run, but then sank down again to the ground beside me.

"Leave him alone, Kaspar," Bertrand slurred. "He can attest that the Jew was already dead when he got here."

Hans didn't seem to hear them.

"Could he be alive? I must see if he's breathing!" he muttered. He stretched out his hand as if to touch me, but then pulled it back quickly. Then—slowly—he stretched out his hand again and rested it against my heart.

Suddenly, the world became brighter than the sun and I had to cover my eyes with my hands. Fire ran through my body. There was just one thought in my mind—I must save my people! When I dropped my hands, the town square was bathed in gentle morning light. And I was there and wasn't there at the same time. I was gone yet I was not gone. I lifted up my hands—stubby fingers with hair on their backs. I ran them over my paunchy stomach and fingered my pockmarked skin. I leaned over the well to catch my reflection in the water . . .

Hans, the journeyman draper, was staring back at me.

What was happening?! I looked like Hans but I felt like me. I *was* me. Me. Natan, son of Simon the Jew. I was never more certain of anything in my entire life. And yet another me was staring back at me from the well water. Natan, with his long fingers and curly hair and upright carriage, was curled up on the ground in eternal sleep. And Hans . . . where did he go?

"Sweet Jesus, what happened here?"

The night watch arrived with Anselm in tow. The watchman was clutching his knife. Did he think that I had committed murder? That *I* had killed *me*?

I opened my mouth to tell him that Kaspar was the guilty one, but then I saw the oaf's malignant stare and thought better of it. "He was like this when I got here," I blurted. "I-I didn't see what happened." I immediately wished that I could take back what I'd said, but it was too late.

"The draper is telling the truth," Kaspar said. "The Jew was throwing garbage into the well when we got to the square. We tried to stop him, but he attacked us with his knife. We had to kill him. There was no other way." He pointed to the weapon he had put into my hand. "See? He is still holding the knife he used against us."

"The other Jews who were with him ran away," Anselm said. He spat on the ground. "Cowards!"

I wanted to challenge what they'd said, but then I reconsidered. Who would take my word over that of Kaspar? He was a Christian and not a hated Jew like me. He was a master butcher, and both respected and feared throughout the city. And even if the night watch would listen to me, what could I say? That Kaspar and his friends had killed me and my soul now resided in the body of Hans? Nobody would believe it. They'd think that the devil had possessed me. I had to come up with a more convincing story if I wanted to save my people. So I decided to keep my own counsel until I could formulate a better plan.

By now, a crowd had gathered around us. The merchant, the tanner, the mason, the knight on his horse, the lady in her litter—all were whispering and pointing at me. At the other me. At the body lying on the ground.

The night watch sent a lad to fetch my parents. Mama and Papa came running. Shmuli was behind them, crying. None of them had even bothered to don their cloaks in the bitter cold. Mama threw herself over my body, keening. Papa dropped to his knees beside her, tears running down his face.

"Natan! Natan! My beautiful boy. What have they done to you?"

I could no longer bear it. I bent over her.

"Don't cry, Mama! Don't be distressed!" I whispered. "I'm here. Still here. Look at your loving Natan, the oldest child of your loins."

She stared into my eyes, and then shuddered and pushed me away. "It cannot be," she whispered.

"Hans, have you no heart?" Papa cried. "Is this your idea of a jest? Leave her alone!"

CHAPTER 7

I t felt strange to see them carry me away on the bier with my parents and Shmuli following. I wanted to go with them, but I knew it couldn't be. I leaned over the edge of the well again. It was still Hans staring back at me.

My head ached abominably. I was going to follow my family home and try once again to explain who I was, but then I remembered how Mama had shuddered and pushed me away. I leaned against the wall of the cathedral to collect my thoughts and decide what to do next. The pain in my head made it difficult to think clearly.

"So, Hans," came a voice. It was the night watch. "Are you certain the Jew was dead when you found him?"

How should I reply? I couldn't tell him that he was addressing a dead man. He'd never believe me.

"He was dead," I said simply.

"Go home," said the watch. "I'll let you know if the Ammeister wishes to speak with you."

I nodded dumbly. Home? There was only one place I could go.

Elena was weeping in her bedchamber. When she saw me, she ran up and clutched my arm.

"Oh, Hans! He is dead! My beautiful Natan is with the angels," she cried. "This is my punishment for our secret meetings."

She sank down into a chair. I sat down across from her and pressed her hands into mine.

"I'm not gone, my love. Your Natan is still here," I whispered into her ear. "Look into my eyes."

She seemed horrified. "W-what do you mean?!"

"Look at me, Elena," I insisted. "Look at me!"

Our gazes locked. A tremor ran through her body, and she tore her hand from my grasp. She ran to the doorway and drew apart the drapes hanging over it.

"Get out!" she shouted. "Get out, Hans! I don't understand why you're behaving so strangely!"

"I'm not Hans," I spluttered.

"I don't understand what you mean."

"I am not Hans!" I repeated.

"Of course you are! You have Hans's face, his hands, his body, his voice. You *are* Hans!"

"No, I'm not!" I insisted.

"Then w-who are y-you?"

"It's me, Elena," I said softly. "It's me. It's Natan."

She turned her head away, but before she did, I noticed that her eyes were glistening with tears. "You're full of lies!"

I stepped even closer. "It's me, Natan, standing before you. It's me, Natan, loving you, as I always have. Please believe me. Please. I'm the Natan who met you last night when the cathedral bell rang twelve times. The Natan who told you that he loved you. And do you remember what else I told you? That nothing can keep us apart. Well, here I am, Elena."

Then I recounted what had happened on my way home, and everything that followed.

Her fist was clasped to her mouth and her eyes became dark pools of confusion. "I don't believe you."

"But you must! You must realize that I could never have come up with such an incredible tale if it wasn't the truth. Why would I?"

She was silent, her eyes tightly shut. Finally, she opened them and peered at me.

"Dear Mother of God," she whispered. "If you're telling the truth, where did you and I meet last night?"

"I came to your house. After you opened the gate in the fence behind the garden, we sat and talked in the kitchen, as always."

"Why did you come to me?"

"You sent me a missive. You said you had to see me immediately. When I arrived, you told me about the destruction of the Jews in the cities of Bern and Zofingen, and how Ammeister Schwarber had refused to mete out the same fate to the Jews of Strasbourg."

She became so pale that I feared she would lose her senses.

"It is you," she whispered. "It must really be you. Nobody else would know what you just told me."

"Are you all right? Shall I fetch your father?"

She walked over to me and ran her fingers over my lank hair and my sallow skin. Her touch was as light as a feather. Then she fell into a dead faint.

ELENA'S STORY

CHAPTER 8

I awoke to the sound of his voice calling my name. He dabbed my brow with a damp cloth and warmed my fingers between his hands.

"You finally regained your senses! You frightened me so much, Elena!" he cried.

He gathered me in his arms. His hands felt clammy and his hair was greasy against my cheeks.

"What a fool I was to tell you such news so suddenly," he said. "But I needed you to know it's me, my love. It's your Natan. You are the sun warming my face and the moon guarding my sleep. I couldn't bear it if you didn't recognize me."

I disengaged myself as gently as I could. My skin crawled at his touch and all I could see when I looked at him were his yellow teeth and his soft paunch. Where was the curly hair I used to run my fingers through? Where were the long, tapered fingers that I loved to feel against my skin?

His voice sounded like the voice of Hans, but he spoke as Natan spoke, with the words of a poet. He looked like Hans, but he knew things only my Natan could know. I forced myself to look into his eyes and felt his love surround me. I was finally certain that I was gazing into the eyes of my beloved. There could be no doubt about that.

I forced myself to reach out and touch his hand. "I believe you. You *are* Natan. But I don't understand how you can be both alive and dead, both you and not you. And what has become of Hans?"

"I don't understand it myself, my love. Somehow, in the moment of death, I entered Hans's body. I have heard some of the men at our synagogue talk of such things, but I never believed them to be true."

I thought for a long moment before speaking. "I can see that I must be satisfied with your answer for now. But what shall we do?"

A sigh of relief escaped his lips. "We must tell the Ammeister what befell me. We must convince him that my people are innocent of the terrible crime they stand accused of."

"How can we do that? He'll think that an evil spirit possessed you, that it's the devil speaking through your lips."

"It's not the devil who kept me among the living even after I died," he said quietly.

He lifted his head and looked to the heavens without uttering another word. He didn't have to. I crossed myself. I knew who he was talking about.

"I must make Peter Schwarber believe me somehow," he muttered.

"Is there no one who can help you?"

He was lost in thought for a moment, then he jumped up from the bench, grabbed my hands and danced me around the chamber. "Not only are you beautiful, my love, but you're also wise!"

"What did I say?" I laughed.

"I'll go and see Rabbi Weltner. He's very learned. He'll understand what has happened and will tell me what to do."

"Shall we talk to my father first? He is wise and will help us."

He dropped my hands. "No, we mustn't. If my own parents didn't believe it was me, your father will be no different. My only hope is Rabbi Weltner. He is well versed in Jewish mysticism, or what we call Kabbalah. He will know what has happened to me."

"I'll come with you to see him . . . uh, Natan."

"Absolutely not," he said. "I don't want to involve you in my troubles."

It was so strange to hear Natan's words coming out

of Hans's mouth.

"I'm already involved," I said firmly, "and I insist you let me help you."

"People might look askance at a Christian girl like you in the Street of the Jews."

"I don't care. I'm coming with you, Hans." I clapped my hand over my lips. "I mean Natan! I'm sorry. Please forgive me."

I followed him to the street. When we reached Judenstrasse, I pulled the hood of my cloak low over my face in case I met someone I knew. I didn't want anybody to see me on the Street of the Jews. They would wonder what I was doing there.

NATAN'S STORY

CHAPTER 9

I clasped my hands together in my lap and willed my heart to slow as I gazed at Rabbi Weltner on the opposite side of the table. Elena was next to me and I could see by the grayness of her complexion that she shared my fears. The rabbi kept twirling his long white beard around his finger.

"Yes, yes," he mumbled, as if talking to himself, "I have read of such a thing."

He turned and took a roll of parchment off a shelf on the wall, unrolling it reverently and smoothing it on the table. I tried to make out the Hebrew words, but they were upside down. The rabbi ran his finger down the page until he reached the part he wanted. He began to read to himself with his lips moving.

Finally, he murmured, "Just as I thought!" He rolled up the parchment and put it back where he'd found it, then leaned toward me, his face full of wonder. "You, Natan, are an *ibbur*."

I must have looked bewildered, for the smile of satisfaction slowly left the old man's face.

"An *ibbur*," he prompted. "This occurs when a righteous person's soul takes up residence in another's body. Your soul, Natan, has left your body and migrated into the body of Hans the draper."

My mind went blank. I had to repeat his words to myself before they made any sense.

"With due respect, my rabbi, why would I do such a thing? Why would my soul enter Hans's body?"

"It happens when someone's time here on this earth ends before he can fulfill a promise or complete a task important to our people. Before you were killed, you were unable to warn the Ammeister that the Jews of Strasbourg did not poison the communal well to cause the Great Pestilence. It is Hashem's will that you save our people from the false accusations being made against them. Without doubt, the fate of the Jews in our city rests in your hands. You must convince Ammeister Schwarber and his council of the truth."

"And if I'm successful?" I asked. "If I complete my task, what becomes of me then?"

The rabbi shifted uneasily in his seat. "Don't ask me such questions, Natan, I beg of you."

"Please, Rabbi Weltner, tell me the whole truth. Will I have to live the rest of my life in the body of Hans?"

The rabbi's eyes filled with tears. It told me all I needed to know.

I took a deep breath, but I felt a new resolve to discharge my duty. "All right, I must make the Ammeister understand that my people pose no threat to Strasbourg. But how? Nobody will believe that I am Natan and not Hans. They'll say that I've been possessed by the devil, and that my words are the devil's words."

"You must make them believe you. The situation for Jews in this city is growing worse by the hour. A few days ago, Ammeister Schwarber ordered the torture of several men in our community to prove to the Christian citizens that no righteous person would confess to spreading the Black Death, no matter the agony he suffered. Baruch Hashem, all the men maintained their innocence. But the Ammeister's actions prove how desperate he's becoming."

He stopped talking for a moment and looked at Elena before continuing.

"I too only believed you because Elena vouched for your claims. Unfortunately, if it becomes known that you are not Hans but Natan, you could both be in grave danger. As you well know, the friendship between the two of you is against the law. Elena shouldn't help you again—at least not outside the confines of this room."

Elena blushed deeply at the disapproval in his face.

"I told Natan that we should talk to my papa and tell him the truth," Elena cried. "He'll speak to Ammeister Schwarber on our behalf."

"I wouldn't advise it," Rabbi Weltner said. "Even if your father accepts that Natan has somehow taken over Hans's body—which, as a Christian, he will not be disposed to do—he will be furious about your relationship with the son of Simon the Jew."

"But my papa is a just and fair man who treats everyone equally. He doesn't hate anybody," Elena countered.

"You're his daughter," said the rabbi, smiling sadly. "Believe me, I know what I'm talking about. You wouldn't be doing your father a favor by involving him in Natan's predicament."

Elena fell silent. Rabbi Weltner turned to me again.

"I have had dealings with the Ammeister in the past about the fines levied against us in return for his protection. I've always found him to be tolerant and a man of his word. I'll try to arrange an interview for you with him."

"Thank you, Rabbi." I bowed deeply.

"Natan," he said, taking my hand in his and looking earnestly at my face, "you must understand that the future of our people rests upon your shoulders."

I nodded. "I'll strive somehow to make the Ammeister listen to me, I promise. But first, I must go to my parents and convince them that I'm still among the living. Can you come with me? They're more likely to listen to you."

"I'll go with you to see your parents, Natan, but you must accept that you aren't among the living. Not really." A deep sadness suffused Rabbi Weltner's face.

From the corner of my eye, I saw Elena's shoulders slump. I turned to her and said, "You must come too. You give me great courage."

She smiled sweetly, pulled the hood of her cloak low over her face and followed us into the street.

Mama's eyes grew larger as Rabbi Weltner patiently explained that I had become an *ibbur*. My father's face turned scarlet, and I feared that he would suffer an attack of apoplexy.

"Do you take us for fools, Rabbi?" he roared. "Do you expect us to believe that our son's spirit took over this Christian?" He pointed an angry finger at me.

"I too find it most strange that Natan occupied the body of a person who isn't one of us. The only explanation I can offer is that Hans must number Jews among his ancestors, perhaps unbeknownst even to himself."

"Please listen to our rabbi, Papa!" I pleaded.

"Don't call me 'Papa'!" he raged.

I took a step toward him and lowered my voice. "It's me," I began. "It's your son talking to you—the son who learns with you every Shabbos, who folds the clothes you buy and loads them into your cart to sell. The son who found you broken and beaten in the alley. Who stayed by your bedside for three days with Mama, cooling your feverish brow and applying poultices to your wounded skin."

My father turned his head away, but my mother drew closer. She ran her fingers over my face like a blind woman. I stood very still, afraid even to breathe.

"Could it possibly be?" she whispered. "Simon, what if Hans and the rabbi are telling the truth?" She grasped my father's hand and put it against my face. "Don't you understand what this means? Our Natan is still alive!"

But Papa tore his fingers away as if bitten by a rabid dog. "Don't be foolish, woman!" he cried.

"No! No!" the rabbi said. "You misunderstood my words, mistress. I never said that your son lives. It's only his soul that has moved into the body of another."

I began to entreat them again. "Please, Mama. Please, Papa. You know your own son!"

"Listen, Hans, do you think my brain is addled?" my father growled. "You don't look like my son. You don't sound like my son. You're *not* my son! Stop this nonsense and let my poor Natan rest in peace."

"But it's me, Papa," I insisted. "It's another me!" But I knew my pleas were to no avail.

"Out with you, you spawn of the devil!" my father cried, pointing to the doorway. "You might have fooled the rabbi with your wily tricks, but you can't fool me. You have your nerve coming to my house with your lies and bringing this foolish young girl with you. Get out of here! All of you!"

Elena took my hand and squeezed my fingers.

"You father is so full of grief that he doesn't know what he is saying," she murmured. "You must forgive him."

"He's usually such a kind man," the rabbi observed.

"Please, Simon," Mama implored, her eyes brimming with tears. "They might be telling the truth! If they are, we still have our Natan with us!" She looked at me with sad eyes. "Or at least part of him."

"Don't be foolish, woman!" my father snapped. "In another few hours our Natan will be in the ground for eternity, and we will never see him again."

Pain and grief tore at my heart. I wanted to howl, to cry, to tear my hair, but I remained silent.

Papa sank down to the bench by the table and dropped his head into his arms. "Get out of my house," he repeated in a muffled tone.

"You'd better do as he asks," my mother said. "He is stubborn as a mule. He won't listen to you once he has made up his mind."

"Do you believe me, Mama?"

She fixed her eyes on the rushes covering the floor and moved them about with the toe of her slipper to stall for time. She would not meet my gaze. She clasped her hands together as if in prayer, before finally whispering, "I don't know what to believe."

I couldn't help sighing—a sigh that shattered the silence more than any words possibly could. My feet felt fixed to the floor, but somehow I followed Elena and the rabbi out of the house.

Shmuli was out front, drawing circles in the dirt with a twig. I stooped down beside him and lifted his chin, then pressed a sweetmeat into his hand.

"Thank thee," he mumbled, staring at me through red-rimmed eyes. "Who are you?"

The pain in my heart sealed my lips.

"Nobody you'd know," I was finally able to mutter.

Elena and I stood concealed behind a large tree in the Jewish cemetery. Her warmth against my body comforted me. It was so cold that the tears running down her cheeks became shining crystals on her face. I wanted to cry too, but all my tears had dried up.

We peeked around the trunk of the tree as the plain wooden coffin holding my body was lowered into the grave. My heart was beating so fast that I could hardly breathe. I was standing next to my beloved and being lowered into my grave at the same time. What would happen to me?

The thought of my body lying in the cold earth was too dreadful to contemplate. Every shovelful of dirt hitting the casket was like a fist to my belly. As I watched my father and our neighbors filling the grave with soil, I thought back to the question Rabbi Weltner had refused to answer. I ran my fingers over my squat frame. The soft creature I had become was all that was left. He had forever replaced the Natan I had once been. Again I thought of Hans. Where did he go? Would he ever come back? And if he did, what would happen to me?

My mother had to be held back by two strong men to prevent her from jumping into the grave after me, but finally it was over. My body had disappeared under a mound of cold earth. I rubbed my eyes with Hans's fingers and wiped the drip from my nose with the back of Hans's hand. Mama and Papa left the cemetery shrouded in grief. The other mourners followed behind. Finally, there were only the two of us left. We decided to go home. There was nothing else for us to do.

Elena once again visited me in my dreams that night. She was standing across from me, with only the mortal hole and the mound of earth next to it separating us. She was weeping, unchecked tears rolling down her cheeks and her eyes fixed on my grave.

"Don't cry, Elena. I'm still here. Look at me! Your Natan is with you. I will never leave you."

Her eyes remained on the grave.

"Elena!" I cried. "Elena! It's me—your Natan."

She lifted her head and stared in my direction with unseeing eyes. She cupped her ear and listened intently, but then shook her head and walked away.

I stood there, dumbfounded, staring after her.

ELENA'S STORY

CHAPTER 10

"**T**his is the fabric I want!" exclaimed Gerda, pointing to a bolt of crimson silk.

"I wouldn't recommend such a bright shade to a lady with your high color, mistress," said Natan.

I was signaling him behind Gerda's back to be quiet, but he merely stared at me in puzzlement.

"Are you suggesting that my complexion is too ruddy?" Gerda sniffed. "How dare you insult me so! I don't want to deal with a rude oaf like you. From now on, I will purchase my silks at Master Adolf's shop, where they know how to treat their customers."

Before Natan or I could reply, she rolled out of the store with her purse still full of jangling coins.

Unfortunately, my father heard the entire exchange. Although he rarely lost his temper, this time he gave in to his feelings.

"Have you lost your senses, Hans?!" he thundered. "Did you forget everything I have ever taught you? Your job is to sell our merchandise, not to discourage our customers from buying it!"

Natan's ears became as crimson as the silk he had refused to sell to Gerda. He began to stammer apologies under his breath. I was quick to interrupt him.

"Leave Hans alone, Father! He works day and night to promote your interests. He's exhausted. And finding that dead Jew in the town square two nights ago must still prey on his mind."

Father seemed surprised at my spirited defense of his journeyman, for I usually ignored Hans.

"I'll admit that you're a hard worker, Hans, but I don't know what has got into you. Yesterday, you couldn't tell the difference between silk from Byzantium and silk spun on the isle of Sicily. Today, you insult a customer with great wealth. When I talk to you, it's as if I'm speaking to a different person."

I was tempted to explain that Hans had indeed become a different person, but then I remembered Rabbi Weltner's warning not to involve my papa in Natan's problems.

"Hans has been working too hard, Father," I said. "He deserves time away from the shop."

Papa nodded. "You may have a free day, Hans," he said. "But one day only. And I expect the old Hans back tomorrow."

I rubbed my eyes. "I didn't sleep well last night, Father. I couldn't get the dead Jew out of my mind either. I kept dreaming about him. Can I also have some time away from the shop?"

"Idle hands are the devil's tools," Papa declared in a sanctimonious tone.

"Who is idle? I want to visit Mother, that's all. I haven't been to her grave for weeks."

I had lost my dear mother when she brought me into the world, a wailing, puny infant. Papa told me that only the devotion of my wet nurse, Vera—the woman who was now our cook—had saved me from following my mama into the arms of Jesus.

Papa became misty-eyed, as he always did when my mother was mentioned. And as always, I pretended not to notice. I felt terrible lying to him, but I certainly couldn't tell him that I needed time off work to go to the Ammeister's office with Natan. Rabbi Weltner had arranged for us to see Peter Schwarber.

"Don't forget to take flowers to the grave," he said in a gruff voice before leaving the room.

"The Ammeister will never believe me," Natan said as we crossed the square toward the town hall. It was an ugly, squat building with a peaked roof, and it housed not only Peter Schwarber's office but also the chamber of the city council. "I wouldn't believe it either if somebody told me that he was a ghost inhabiting the body of another person," he continued. "I'd think that anybody making such a claim was possessed by the devil."

"Well, you must make the Ammeister believe you."

"There is no way I can," he said miserably.

Suddenly, he grabbed my hand and pulled me behind a cart filled with hides and furs of all kinds. Its owner was in animated conversation with two other men and didn't notice us.

"What's the matter?" I asked.

"Shh! Look!" Natan pointed toward the steps in front of the town hall. A tall man with red hair and a goatee was leaving the building with two other men. "That's Kaspar! The beast who murdered me! The other two were with him at the well."

"Are you sure?"

"I could never forget his ugly face."

Kaspar and his companions were laughing and jostling each other as they headed in our direction. In a moment, they were close enough that we could hear them talking.

"That went well!" one of them gloated.

"Better than I expected. I can't believe how easy it was to convince the Ammeister and his councilors that the Jews poisoned the well in the town square," Kaspar said, snickering. "A pox upon the Jews! Let them try to talk their way out of this predicament."

When they'd passed us, Natan and I just stared at each other.

"It's even worse than I thought," he finally said. "It's obvious that I can't tell the Ammeister what really happened—not after Kaspar filled his head with his lies." Panic spread across his face. "What should I say instead?"

I thought deep and hard. He was right. We needed a more plausible explanation.

"We must come up with a story that Peter Schwarber will believe. A story that will prove to him that Kaspar and his accomplices are murdering brutes. Why don't you tell the Ammeister that you saw Kaspar poisoning the well without revealing to him that you're really Natan?"

He thought for a moment. "That could work," he agreed. "But what about the murder? How do I explain my body on the ground?" Tears filled his eyes as he spoke.

I wanted to cry myself at the thought of my beautiful Natan cold as the frozen earth. I shook my head to remind myself that my lost love was standing in front of me, full of grief. I knew that I should put my arms around him and tell him that I loved him, but I couldn't bring myself to do it. The thought of his pockmarked face against mine and his greasy hair twirled around my fingers filled me with revulsion.

Instead, I forced myself to punch his arm genially. "Just tell Schwarber that you witnessed the murder," I said. "He'll believe that."

"I hope so," he replied wearily as we mounted the steps at the town hall.

We waited for an hour on hard benches. Finally, a clerk escorted us into the council chamber. Instead of being greeted by the tall, powerful figure of Peter Schwarber, as we'd expected, we found the entire council staring back at us. The Ammeister was sitting at the head of a long table, leaning back in a carved chair that looked like a throne. He was surrounded by the master tradesmen who made up the council. They occupied long wooden benches. A large crest of the city was hanging on the wall behind them.

Schwarber motioned us to come into the room. It felt as if a thousand eyes were boring into us. Suddenly, my courage deserted me and I felt like fleeing. Natan must have felt me tensing, for he took my hand and drew me into the chamber after him. Schwarber asked us to come closer to the table. There was no question of disobeying him.

"Who are you?" he asked. "Why are you here?"

Natan bowed deeply. I followed his example and curtsied.

"I'm Hans, a journeyman draper. My master is Wilhelm," he said. "I'm a member of the drapers' guild."

"And I'm Elena, the daughter of Wilhelm," I added.

The Ammeister leaned toward us. "I know your father, mistress. Wilhelm is an honorable man," he remarked in his deep, sonorous voice. "What brings you before us?"

"My tale is long and difficult to comprehend, but every word of it is true," Natan began. "Three nights ago, I was crossing the town square when the church bells rang a dozen times. I saw several figures in the distance. Being of rather small stature"—his pudgy hands pointed to his short, squat body, drawing laughter from several councilors—"I knew that I was no match for them, so I hid in the shadows cast by the cathedral walls. I could still see everything that was going on." He took a deep breath and then continued. "There were three of them, and one of them was dragging a body over the icy cobblestones. The same man was also holding a squirming white cat under his arm. The other two were carrying sacks over their shoulders."

The councilors began to murmur among themselves. Schwarber banged the table with a wooden gavel to restore order.

"You're doing well," I whispered to Natan. "You've captured their attention."

Please God, I silently prayed, let me have given him the right advice.

"Silence!" Schwarber cried. "Silence!"

The councilors stopped talking and Natan resumed his tale.

"Not only could I see the three men, but I could also hear them talking," he said.

"Had you ever seen these men before?" asked one of the councilors. He was Adolf the draper, my father's chief competitor. Papa always maintained that he wasn't an honest man.

"Yes, I had," Natan answered without hesitation. I was proud of the way he met Adolf's eyes. "All three are always loitering in the town square. The man dragging the body on the ground was the butcher, Kaspar. You must know him too. He is a great, hulking oaf with red hair and a goatee. He has a shop in Butchers' Lane."

Several council members nodded.

"What happened next?" Ammeister Schwarber asked.

Natan shot me a quick glance. I nodded in encouragement and he resumed speaking.

"The most incredible thing," he said. "Kaspar let go of the body and it fell to the cobblestones with a thud. As it was lying on the ground, it began to moan. Kaspar and his henchmen backed away in panic.

"'He's still alive!' one of the culprits said. He was slurring his words as if drunk.

"'Not for long!' Kaspar cried.

"He drew his knife and plunged it deep into the man's chest. There was a gurgling noise, then silence.

"'Good riddance!' he said. In the moonlight I could see a big glob of his spit land on the dead man's face.

"Kaspar then turned to his accomplices and ordered them to empty their sacks into the well. I could smell feces and garbage as they obeyed him without question. The mewing white cat was the last object to be thrown in."

The councilors were spellbound. Natan paused for a moment to wipe his brow with his sleeve.

"What then?" Schwarber asked.

"Kaspar clapped his hands. He said, 'Good! Let the Jews try to explain this.' His laughter made the hair on my neck stand up. He sent his friend to get the night watch and said they would tell everybody that they came upon a group of Jews while they were poisoning the well. 'We'll say that we caught only this lone cur,' he directed. 'When we tell people that this Jew tried to attack us, they'll call us heroes.' He crouched down and put his knife into the Jew's hand, wrapping the dead man's fingers around the handle.

"I was so frightened that I was afraid to breathe. I crept around the side of the cathedral and went back into the square. As I approached Kaspar and his accomplice, I began to sing as if I too were drunk. The rest of the tale you already know. They told me the same lying story they told the night watch when he arrived."

Natan stopped speaking and looked at the councilors expectantly, but nobody asked any questions. It was so quiet in the chamber that you could have heard a pin drop.

"Ammeister and honored councilors," Natan resumed, "the next day I heard rumors on the streets that these three men were claiming it was the Jews of our city who poisoned the well to bring the Great Pestilence upon us. That's a complete lie! I saw Kaspar and his friends do the deed with my own eyes. The Jews are innocent! I had to step forward and tell you the truth, even though I fear Kaspar's revenge when he hears that I told you what he did."

He bowed and fell silent again. This time, excited chatter broke out among the councilors.

Adolf the draper broke into raucous laughter. "I don't believe a word you say. Are you in your cups or have demons taken hold of your brain?" He pointed an accusing finger at Natan. "How dare you waste our time with such a foolish, lying tale. Kaspar said that you told the night watch the Jew was already dead when you came upon him."

"I didn't have a choice, master. The night watch would never have believed me. After all, it was Kaspar's man who fetched him. But I knew that for justice to be done, I would eventually have to tell the true events to you, most honored councilors, and to the Ammeister."

"Stop your lies!" Adolf cried. "Brother Kaspar told us a short time ago that he saw the Jews poisoning the well."

"But, master, that's simply not true! I saw Kaspar poison the well and kill the Jew with my own eyes. You must believe me. I have nothing to gain by telling you such a story. I only want justice done."

"It's your word against Kaspar's. Why should we listen to your defense of lying Jews?" Adolf sneered. "I'm convinced that Kaspar the butcher is telling the truth."

Before Natan could even reply, the Ammeister once again banged the table with his gavel.

"Gentlemen, let's consider both stories. Kaspar says the Jews poisoned the well, and Hans here says they did not. It is true that Kaspar could have poisoned the well himself to make the Jews look guilty. But what reason would the Jews have to taint the water? They depend upon it for drinking, just as we do. And I remind you that not one of the Jews we had put on the wheel confessed to the poisoning."

"The Jews don't die from the pestilence like the rest of us," Adolf said.

"That's true," Felix the barber replied. "It is said that they die at half the rate we do. I have heard they made a pact with the devil to protect themselves."

All the councilors began to murmur and debate.

Ammeister Schwarber cleared his throat. "Does anybody have any questions to ask?"

Here was my opportunity to speak up. "May I address the councilors, Ammeister?"

"Please, mistress," he replied. "Try to talk some sense into their foolish heads."

"Councilors," I began, "you must listen to Hans. He is the most truthful person you'll ever meet—truthful to a fault. I have never heard him utter a single lie."

I stopped speaking for a moment to make sure that I had the entire council's attention. The bold gaze of several of the men made me shudder, but I forced myself to continue.

"If Hans tells you that the Jews are innocent, they are innocent. If he tells you that Kaspar the butcher poisoned the well and murdered Natan, then that's what happened. Other than Kaspar's wrath, he has nothing to gain by defending the Jews. You must believe that." I curtsied deeply and fixed my eyes on the floor, not uttering another word. I clasped my hands to hide their trembling.

"But, mistress," Adolf said, "the Jews are—"

"Silence, Adolf," Schwarber said, cutting off his words.

The draper glared at him but stopped talking.

"Thank thee, mistress," said the Ammeister, turning to me. "And also our thanks to you, Hans. You may now excuse yourselves from the chamber. We have much to discuss. We will let you know whose version of events we believe—yours or Kaspar's. Only one of you can be telling the truth."

CHAPTER 11

Vera and I were heading down Butchers' Lane the next morn to purchase meat she would bake into delicious pies. Just thinking about them made my mouth water. The shops had all kinds of pork, mutton and hens hanging from great hooks in their windows. The smell of blood was thick in the air and I could feel the bile rising in my throat. I pressed my sleeve against my nose to keep the fumes away but without much success.

"Let's go to Heinrich's shop today," Vera said. "He tries to charge me too much, but then they all do. At least I always find his meat fresh."

When we finally arrived at Heinrich's, we found him preoccupied with a huge slab of meat he was cutting. When he saw us, he put down his cleaver and wiped his hands on his bloody apron.

"What can I do for you, Mother?" he asked Vera.

The rounded shape of his stomach declared to the world that he loved his own merchandise.

"We're here to buy pork and a hare," Vera said. "Do you have nice meat for us?"

"The best meat in all of Butchers' Lane," he boasted.

Vera snorted. I could barely make sense of the rapid dickering that followed until coins changed hands to the satisfied smiles of both participants. The butcher dropped the hare and the large slabs of pork into the baskets on our arms.

"Time to go home," I said to Vera as we linked hands and set out through the throng of humanity surrounding us.

"Your papa will be happy with the pork we bought," she said. "He is a man who likes his meat."

"It's not the meat he cares for but the delicious way you cook it. Father says you make the best pies in the city."

"Why are you trying to turn my head with your nonsense?" she scolded. But I could see by her grin that she was pleased.

"I'm just telling the truth!"

"I know your papa likes . . ." Her voice trailed off as our path was suddenly blocked by a redheaded giant with a goatee. It was Kaspar. The people surrounding us gave him a wide berth. My hands became clammy and I began to tremble. I prayed that I wouldn't lose my senses.

"So, my pretty, what are you doing in Butchers' Lane?" Kaspar asked.

"Let us pass." I made sure I didn't allow my fear to show in my voice.

"Don't you want Kaspar to show you a good time?" His eyes roamed over my body, filling me with dread.

I tried to duck around him, but he grabbed my arm. When I twisted away, he tightened his grasp and pulled me closer.

"Let me go!"

"You know better than to cross Kaspar, wench!" he said. "Come with me to my shop." He pulled me so close that I could smell his foul breath on my face. "I'll give you something there you'll never forget!"

"Have you lost your senses, Kaspar?" Vera cried. "The wrath of Wilhelm the draper will reach far if you insult his daughter!"

"Insult her? Your high-and-mighty master should feel honored that an esteemed guild member like me is interested in his whelp."

"Whelp? How dare you!" I tried to pry his fingers off my arm.

His laughter at my puny efforts reduced me to tears.

"Let my mistress go!" Vera cried. "I've had enough of your cheek."

"Go home, Mother. Your mistress doesn't need you here. She has more important things to do."

In the blink of an eye, Vera pushed me so hard that I fell. Kaspar was startled and let go of my arm. Before he knew what was happening, Vera had picked up the hare in her basket and swung it at his midsection. The butcher let out an agonized roar and fell to the ground, clutching his private parts.

Vera pulled me up from the cobblestones. "Run!" she cried. "Run!" We set off at full speed, the hare still clutched in Vera's hand. The crowd around us parted as the Red Sea must have parted before the ancient Hebrews escaping slavery in Egypt.

"You'll pay for this!" Kaspar roared. "Nobody makes a fool of me!"

We were out of breath by the time we arrived home. I was happier to see the shop sign hanging from the eaves than I had ever been to see anything before.

"Your papa will be furious when he hears about Kaspar," Vera said.

"I won't tell Papa what happened. And I want your oath that you won't either."

"Why not?"

"Kaspar is dangerous. He's strong as a bull and evil as well. Father is no longer young. If he confronts Kaspar, he'll get hurt. Promise me that you won't tell him!"

Vera thought for a long moment. Finally she said, "It's not right for Kaspar to go unpunished, but I don't want your papa hurt. I won't say a word."

She went to the kitchen and began to skin the hare, but I noticed that she wasn't singing while she worked, as was her habit.

As the sun dipped below the horizon, Heinrich the butcher appeared at our shop's window. Fortunately, I was by myself, without customers or my father in sight.

Heinrich plunked down the two baskets of meat Vera and I had left behind.

"I've brought your meat," he said. "Don't come to Butchers' Lane for the next few weeks. I'll bring your meat to your house. You don't want to run into Kaspar by chance."

He pushed my thanks aside. As he was leaving, he turned back and offered an encouraging smile.

"Several of the butchers in our guild have been cheated by Kaspar," he said. "None of them had the courage to stand up to him, but you and your servant did." He chuckled. "An old woman and a young girl! What's the world coming to?"

—#—

Vera made a fragrant stew of the hare.

"Something smells wonderful," Papa said, sniffing appreciatively as he settled down at the supper table. He sopped up the stew with a thick slab of dark bread.

Vera smiled modestly. "Heinrich's meat is always fresh."

Natan entered the room and walked straight to the wooden bowl we always kept filled with water for cleaning. He dipped his hands in and seemed to be splashing around in it before he sat down beside me.

"What's with all your hand-washing, Hans? You seem to be doing it all the time lately," Papa asked. "Too much washing will unbalance the humors in your body and you will become sick."

Natan smiled but didn't answer him. "What's for dinner?" he asked. "I'm famished!"

"Can't you smell it?" Papa said. "Vera cooked us hare."

A look of distaste flitted across Natan's features.

"I don't eat hare!"

"What are you talking about, Hans?" Vera asked. "I remember you telling me that it's your favorite dish."

Natan clutched his stomach. He swallowed hard. "I just mean I can't eat it tonight. My stomach is upset. I'll stick to the bread."

"Are you sure?" Papa said. "Vera's hare is the best!"

"I'm sure," Natan mumbled.

He remained quiet for the rest of the meal.

After supper, when everybody else had left the table, I asked if anything was bothering him.

He rubbed his stomach. "I'm hungry."

"You should have eaten some of the hare."

He smiled ruefully. "I couldn't. It's one of the animals we're not allowed to eat."

"Why?"

"The Torah tells us that we may only eat animals that have cloven hoofs and chew their cud, and the hare is not one of those."

"And the hand-washing?" I asked. "Is that a part of your religion as well?"

He nodded. "I didn't think you'd noticed."

"It would be difficult not to. But you should be careful, for my papa is right—too much washing will unbalance the humors in your body. I don't want you in your sickbed."

"I'm glad that you care enough to worry about me." He grinned. "I bet you didn't realize that I also say silent prayers before I eat your bread or drink your father's ale."

"I didn't, but I'll watch you more closely in the future."

"That's fine with me—as long as your father doesn't!"

CHAPTER 12

The pails of water dangling from our hands weighed us down as we made our way back to Papa's shop. Ever since the well in the town square was poisoned, we'd had to fetch our water from the River Ill. I was pleased that Natan had fallen into the habit of accompanying me every day. These were the only times we were alone to discuss our problems. Natan was worried that we still hadn't heard from the Ammeister.

"Surely the councilors must have decided by now who is responsible for poisoning the well—my people or that lying Kaspar and his accomplices," he said. "I keep thinking that I should have told the council the truth about Kaspar and what he did to me."

I chose my words carefully. "If you had told the councilors that you're really Natan and not Hans, they would have said you're possessed by the devil. No, you did right to say what you did. That was the only chance you had to prove that Kaspar is a liar and your people are innocent."

"They still didn't believe me. If they had, Peter Schwarber would have told us by now."

"You're most likely right. If you don't hear from the Ammeister in the next few days, we should tell my father the truth. He'll intercede on your behalf. I'm sure that Schwarber will tell him the council's verdict."

"I don't think we should say anything to your father, at least not yet," he said. "Remember what Rabbi Weltner said—we wouldn't be doing your father a favor by involving him in my problems." He sighed heavily. "Let's wait a little longer. I prefer for him not to know."

He picked up his steps. I trudged after him, straining at the weight of the pails and perspiring despite a temperature so cold that I could see my breath. We passed a group of burghers, most of whom were customers in our shop.

"Good day to you, Hans," one of them called.

Natan didn't look up or respond.

I plucked his arm, causing him to spill some of his water. He glared at me.

"Pay attention, Hans," I berated him. "Fritz the bricklayer is waiting for your greeting. You're behaving

as if you've never seen him before. You must remember how often he comes into our shop!"

Understanding flashed across Natan's face and he
turned to the bricklayer with a wide grin.

"Of course I do," he said. "Good day to you, Fritz,"
he added as we passed the men. "These pails are so
heavy that I wasn't paying attention to anything else."

"You have to learn to respond to the name Hans,"
I whispered to him as we turned down a narrow lane
toward home.

"It's difficult to answer to Hans's name when I don't
feel like him," he replied. "I feel like me!"

As we turned the corner, we stopped short. A dozen
street urchins had surrounded an old Gypsy woman
dressed in bright clothes. The waifs were dancing
around the woman and throwing stones at her head.
She was trying to protect herself by covering her face
with her hands. As the children continued their torment, they sang:

Watch the Gypsy brew her potion,
See her pour it in your ale;
Drink it all and you'll lose all motion
And your Maker awaits.

I lowered my pails to the ground, not caring that
some of the water slopped over the rim.

"What do you think you're doing? Leave the Gypsy alone!"

I grabbed the back of one boy's tunic and tried to pull him out of the circle. The other urchins stopped dancing and fell silent. They stared at me sullenly.

The tallest among them, a boy with a dirty face, turned toward me.

"What's the matter, mistress? Why are you worried about the likes of her?" He spat in the woman's direction. "She's probably a witch."

"The Gypsies poisoned our well to bring the plague upon us," lisped a little maid with the face of an angel.

Natan shot me a quick look.

"I was told it was the Jews who'd poisoned the town well," he said.

"They're both responsible," said the older boy. "The Jews and the Gypsies are equally guilty. May their souls rot in hell!"

"Be gone with you!" Natan cried. He shook his fist at the children. "I'm of a mind to send the watch after you." He turned to me. "Go and fetch the watchman and bring him back with you!"

I took but a few steps in the direction of the town hall before the urchins dispersed in all directions. The old woman sank down to the ground, her hands still covering her face. I leaned over her and tried to pull her up from the frozen cobblestones.

"The ground is cold, Mother. You'll catch your death if you don't stand up."

She struggled to her feet and caught my hand, kissing it before I could stop her.

"Mistress, you and this fine young master saved my life," she said. "How can I ever thank you?"

"What happened?" Natan asked. "Why were those children tormenting you so?"

"I was returning to our caravan in the woods beyond your city when those spawns of Satan attacked me." She bent down and picked up a tambourine lying in the snow. After examining it, she threw it back down. "It's beyond repair." She shook her head sadly. "Them devil children wanted to kill me!"

"Oh no! They just don't know any better," I said.

The woman's black eyes glowed in her swarthy face. "You're too innocent, young mistress, to understand the likes of them. May the Great One bless you—and you too, master—for saving me."

Her expression became crafty.

"My name is Nadya. I was in your city to earn a few coins," she said. She picked up the ripped tambourine again and shook it. "I have many mouths to feed." She held out her hand. "Can you help an old woman like me?"

Natan stared at her in surprise. I slipped a coin into her palm and then held out my own hand toward her.

"Tell my fortune, Mother," I said. "I've heard that your people can see into the future."

She pulled my hand toward her and began to trace the lines in my palm. Suddenly, she trembled and dropped my hand.

"Dear Mother of God! May she protect you!"

"What is it? Do you see something of concern?"

"D-don't ask m-me," she stuttered. She took a deep breath and began to speak more calmly. "There is more in heaven and earth than a poor woman like me can understand." She leaned close. "If you ever need my help, young mistress, come to our caravan. Our people will help you. Gypsies like us have long memories. We never forget when a good deed is done to us."

She curtsied deeply with surprising grace and was gone before I could reply.

"I wonder what she saw in my hand that made her run away?" I asked. "Her people are versed in the black arts, they say."

Natan stared after her solemnly but didn't answer my question.

CHAPTER 13

The winter fair was always important to my father. It was the time when he purchased a great deal of our merchandise from drapers who came from as far away as Toledo in the Iberian Peninsula. It was also the time when he sold the visiting merchants a lot of our own goods. I was always pleased when Papa asked me to help him in the tent we set up on the fairground next to the River Ill. He also asked Natan to help him.

After a few hours of work had passed, Papa told me to take a break. He rubbed his stomach. "Delicacies from all over the world can be had for a few coins at the fair."

"I don't care about the food. I want to see the stilt walkers and the fools."

"I'll come with you," Natan said.

He glanced at Papa, afraid that he would stop him. Fortunately, my father was in a jovial mood.

"Go, go!" he said. "You're young only once."

Natan and I wrapped ourselves in our cloaks against the wintry breeze from the river. We had walked but a few steps when a minstrel began to follow us, strumming his lute and singing a melancholy tune:

Under the linden, on the heath
There the bed of us two was,
There you may find
Lovely both broken flowers and grass.

Natan began to smile and strut. I looked around quickly. Did I want the other fairgoers to think I was Hans's beloved? They didn't know he was really Natan in Hans's skin.

We strolled about, admiring the skill of the tumblers. We had just passed the money changer's booth when Natan stepped very close to me. I could see by the desire in his eyes that he was about to kiss me. The cold rays of the winter sun highlighted every mark on his pallid skin. As I searched my mind for a way to cool his ardor, I noticed a bear on a chain in the distance.

"Look!" I pointed. "Let's see the bear dance."

Had it not been so sad to see Natan's face fall, I might have laughed at the sight.

"Play your fiddle," I told the animal trainer when we drew near. "I want to see what your bear can do."

The shaggy-haired ruffian coaxed a lively tune out of his dilapidated instrument, and the bear began to lumber about. I clapped my hands in false gaiety.

Suddenly, without warning, the bear lowered one of his mighty paws onto my shoulder, ripping my cloak. He opened his great jaws as if to swallow me. His teeth were enormous and his spittle ran down my garments. Natan jumped in front of me and pushed the animal away with all his might before his trainer could shorten the leash.

"Down! Down!" the man cried, pulling on the chain around the bear's neck and forcing it onto all fours.

When the animal was subdued, he turned to me.

"I'm so sorry, mistress!" he pleaded. "I assure you he's never done that before!"

Natan began to berate him, but I pulled him away.

"Are you all right?" he asked with concern.

We had already attracted the attention of several fairgoers.

I nodded, tears streaking my face. "Let's go somewhere where I can compose myself."

"Come with me," he said, leading me toward the riverbank.

—⫻—

In the February cold, we were the only visitors on the banks of the river. We walked along the path by the frozen water until we came to some bulrushes. Natan parted them to reveal a clearing by the shore. He sat on a large boulder next to the water and pulled me down beside him. I dried my tears and took a deep breath to calm down.

"We can't stay here for long. My papa needs our help with his customers." I was glad that my voice was calm.

"He'll manage without us for a bit," Natan said. He looked around the riverbank. "This is one of the few places where we can talk without being overheard."

He reached for my hand and started stroking my fingers. His own fingers felt damp and sticky. I pulled my hand away and wiped it surreptitiously on my skirt.

"Is something wrong?" he asked.

"Nothing. I'm just tired." I looked away at the frozen water.

He put his arm around me and pulled me closer. His touch repulsed me. He must have noticed how I had stiffened, because he let me go.

"What's the matter?"

"I've already told you—nothing!"

I closed my eyes. When I couldn't see him, he sounded just like my Natan. But no matter how hard I tried, I couldn't convince myself that he was the same boy I had once loved, the boy I had longed for with every bone in my body.

"You seem distracted," he said. "Is your father working you too hard?"

I shook my head sadly. "I haven't been sleeping soundly because Kaspar keeps interrupting my dreams. I'm also worried that another week has passed and the Ammeister still hasn't contacted you. I don't understand why. He's usually a man of his word."

"His silence is my reply," Natan said.

Suddenly, there was the crunch of twigs being broken and snow being trampled. Natan put a finger to his lips.

"Hush!" he whispered. "There is somebody coming!"

The bulrushes parted and there she was—Natan's mother.

NATAN'S STORY

CHAPTER 14

She didn't realize that I saw her wipe her fingers on her skirt after I touched her. I felt the stiffening of her spine when I embraced her. Did she no longer love me? How could that be? Such a short time ago, she was eager for my kisses. Did she not realize that I was still the same boy she once said she loved?

But then I touched my face with my hands and felt every bump and groove on my skin, and I couldn't blame her.

I feared that she would think I was weak if I told her how difficult it was to be trapped in *his* body with my own thoughts, my own love, my own desires. Would I be trapped in *his* body for the rest of my life? Where was he? And where would I go if he ever returned and claimed his own vessel? I could never tell her my thoughts, though, for I feared her pity. I craved her love—a love she had given so easily to my other self.

Even in the depths of my misery, I heard the sound of approaching footsteps. The bulrushes parted and there was my mother. Her eyes were red and her face blotchy. I couldn't find the right words to say, so I just stared at her. Elena's eyes were like saucers, her fist at her mouth as if to stifle a scream.

"Forgive me for following you, but I had to speak to you," Mama said.

She looked at my face for a long, long moment, as if she wanted to memorize my features. Her gaze roamed over my stocky frame, my ample paunch and my skinny legs. I didn't mind, so long as she kept looking at me.

"Who are you?" she finally whispered. She reached out shyly and touched my pockmarked face. Then she answered her own question. "Your eyes . . . they are my Natan's eyes. Your words are my Natan's words. Rabbi Weltner must have been telling us the truth. You *are* my Natan, the son I gave birth to. The son I raised. The son I buried."

Her hand passed over her eyes as if to obliterate painful memories.

"I'm still here, Mama."

Then I told her everything again. Amazement, horror, resignation—all ran across her face. When I finished speaking, she pulled me close.

"Natan," she said, patting my hair, "you're really my Natan. Baruch Hashem, he returned you to me."

Tears of joy ran down her cheeks. Elena was crying too.

"I'm ashamed," Mama said. "I should have believed you from the start. When you told me in the town square that you were Natan and not Hans, I looked into your eyes and saw you there, but I was afraid. I should have known you right away."

"You know me now. That's all that matters."

She wiped away her tears. "What should I tell your father to make him believe you? When you came home with Rabbi Weltner, your papa was beyond anger. He said that the rabbi must have been possessed by evil spirits to desecrate your memory so. He hasn't gone to synagogue since. I don't know how he'll react if I tell him that I believe your story."

"So don't tell him, Mama. Not yet. There is a right time for everything."

She nodded reluctantly. "You may be right," she said, but I sensed that she wasn't fully convinced.

I kissed her cheek. "I missed you so much."

"And I missed you, my son." She turned to Elena. "Natan is fortunate to have a loyal friend like you. Somebody told me that they saw you watching his funeral with him from behind a tree."

I told her about my visit to Ammeister Schwarber and the council.

"We still don't know if they believed Natan's story or the lies of that murderous Kaspar," Elena said.

Mama smiled bitterly. "You aren't one of us, Elena, so you don't understand. Jews like us, we can never win. I agree with Natan that the silence of the Ammeister is its own reply." She sighed. "I'm afraid that tough days are facing our people. We are no longer safe in Strasbourg. But where can we go?"

CHAPTER 15

Even though I believed my mother was right, I still felt that I should continue trying to help my people. I decided to visit Rabbi Weltner to ask him to arrange another appointment with the Ammeister. I had to know for sure if the councilors had believed that lying Kaspar over me.

When I arrived at the rabbi's house, he was talking to an older man dressed in country clothes.

"Ah, Hans. Welcome!" he said. "I was just telling Yehuda the peddler about you. Yehuda is from the Mulhouse region. Didn't you once tell me that your family comes from there?"

I had no idea where Hans's family came from, but I couldn't tell that to the rabbi with the peddler hanging on our every word, so I nodded. "I've never been to Mulhouse myself."

"I knew your grandparents well," Yehuda said. "Your grandmother was my wife's cousin once removed. What a pity that both of them departed from our world so young. Your grandfather wasn't of our faith, of course, but he was a most decent man. In them times, a Jew and a Christian could spend their lives together, but that's forbidden nowadays."

My ears perked up. If Hans's grandmother was Jewish, didn't that make him Jewish too?

"My grandmother was Jewish? Nobody ever told me that."

"That she was, as am I. And you?"

"I'm—"

"You and I will talk in a moment, Hans," the rabbi said, throwing me a meaningful glance. "Yehuda must return to his family before the setting of the sun."

With that, he stood up and ushered the man out of the room. I waited for him to come back, my mind racing. It had set my imagination on fire—Hans was one of us!

When Rabbi Weltner returned, he sat down and clasped his hands together in a satisfied manner. "I was right, Natan!" he exulted. "Hans has Jewish ancestors—although perhaps even he doesn't know about them. That's why you were able to settle into his body when you became an *ibbur*." His pleasure dimmed as he took in my drawn and anxious face. He leaned toward me, his eyes reflecting his concern. "How are things? It can't be easy for you."

I choked back my tears. He was the first person to show concern for me. Not even Mama and Elena—both of whom loved me but were caught up in their own grief—realized the pain I was experiencing.

"It's difficult," I acknowledged, "but that's not why I came to see you."

I told him I was concerned that I hadn't heard back from the Ammeister.

"He promised to notify me as soon as the councilors made up their minds. It's been over two weeks and he still hasn't told me which of us the councilors believed."

"I don't understand why Schwarber hasn't contacted you. He is a man of his word. There must be a reason for his silence." He shook his head slowly from side to side. "It's certainly not a good sign."

"What do you advise me to do, Rabbi?"

He stood up and fetched his cloak. "Let's walk down to his office and talk to him now. He never refuses to see me. Peter Schwarber always has time for the Jews of this city."

The same clerk as before met us at the Ammeister's door. He asked us to sit down on the hard benches.

"I'll tell the Ammeister that you're here, Rabbi," he said smarmily. "I'll be just a moment."

"Schwarber will see us right away," the rabbi said to me in a confident tone. "He always does."

The clerk returned a moment later, his expression haughty. "The Ammeister is too busy to talk to you right now," he said shortly. "Come back another time."

Rabbi Weltner was incredulous. "Did you tell him I was the one who wanted to see him?"

"I'm repeating exactly what he said." Gone was his respectful attitude. "Go home, now!"

As we descended the town hall steps, Rabbi Weltner kept repeating, "Something is wrong! Something is wrong! Why wouldn't the Ammeister see us?"

"My mother was right," I said simply. "Jews like us cannot win. Kaspar has won."

"You cannot allow that to happen," the rabbi cried. "You're the only one who can save our people!"

But how was I going to do that?

The next day, Elena and I decided to take a walk to the town square. She wanted to listen to the one of the minstrels who always sang there. When we arrived, however, we found hundreds of people assembled in front of the cathedral. Flags of the different guilds were flying in the breeze. There were also flags bearing the crests of knights and Strasbourg's old noble families.

Peter Schwarber and his councilors were standing on the steps of the cathedral. They were face to face with Kaspar and a dozen burly butchers and tanners, all waving the flags of their guilds.

Kaspar stepped so close to Schwarber that their faces almost touched. "Ammeister, you and your lackeys have had their day!" he shouted. "Master tradesmen like you have too much power over us. It's time that the people ruled our city and not the rich merchants!"

The crowd roared in approval.

"My councilors and I have always been fair and honest!" Schwarber cried over the din. He stepped back from Kaspar.

"That's true," shouted a voice from the crowd. "I can vouch for the Ammeister's good intentions!"

"It's my papa," Elena said. "Why is he here?"

"Isn't he a friend of Peter Schwarber's?" I asked.

Boos rang out from the crowd.

"The Ammeister has the best interests of the people of Strasbourg at heart," Wilhelm continued.

"Silence, old man!" shouted a voice from the mob.

Elena started toward her father, but I held her back. "There is nothing you can do to help him. Your presence might even make his situation worse."

"Ammeister, we've had enough of you and your councilors protecting those who bring the Great Pestilence upon us!" Kaspar bellowed. "The Jews must be expelled from our city, and they must leave behind their ill-gotten gains to be enjoyed by the honest citizens of Strasbourg. What's more, no one should be made to repay the money they lent us at such high rates."

"But . . . but . . . the Jews pay us many pieces of gold to ensure their safety," Schwarber meekly replied.

"Yes, gold that ends up in your hands."

"Liar!" cried the Ammeister with more vigor.

"Who are you calling a liar?" shouted Kaspar, and he slammed his fist into the Ammeister's belly.

Schwarber doubled over and the two men began to grapple. Several fights broke out in the crowd as well.

I put my arm around Elena's shoulders and steered her in the opposite direction. "Time to go home," I said.

She tried to push me away. "I must go to my father!"

"Master Wilhelm can take care of himself. You'd only be in his way."

I felt her relax against me and we fought our way through the pushing, fighting, shouting mob.

As we headed for home, I told Elena about my visit to the Ammeister's office.

"The rabbi was shocked that Schwarber wouldn't see him, but I wasn't surprised. My mother was right— tough times are ahead of us."

"You can't give up so easily!" Elena said. "You must make the Ammeister listen to you."

"That's what Rabbi Weltner said also, but I don't know how."

"You must let me consult my father," she said, wagging a finger in my face. "He'll tell us what to do."

I couldn't think of any other options, so I reluctantly agreed.

We were just turning the corner of Elena's street when a man ran by us. "The Great Pestilence has arrived!" he shouted. "The Great Pestilence is in Strasbourg!"

CHAPTER 16

"Thank God you're home!" Vera cried. "This ain't the time to be gamboling around town. My sister just left. She came to tell me that one of her neighbors sickened with the pestilence." She crossed herself. "He left our world."

"We heard about it on the way home. Who was the unfortunate soul?"

"A traveler from Lake Geneva. My sister says he was a jolly fellow until the sickness took him. He was always ready to laugh and banter, but he was gone in a day. Let's hope that nobody else caught it from him." She stepped closer, wringing her hands. "You must remain inside the house, young mistress, to keep yourself safe!"

"Don't be foolish, Vera," Elena said. "I have things I must do—fetch our water, buy our bread, sell our merchandise."

"I'll do those jobs in your stead."

"I can't be cowering inside the house all the time."

"If you have to go out, young mistress, make sure that you fix your eyes on the ground. Never lock gazes with an afflicted person. His miasma might enter your body through your eyes." She turned to me. "The same goes for you, Hans."

Before I could reply, there was loud banging on the door. When I opened it, Master Wilhelm staggered into the room. He had a cut on his lip and his cloak was torn into shreds. His left eye was bruised and already turning purple. He leaned on my shoulder heavily to keep from falling. I helped him to a bench.

"You're hurt, Papa!" Elena dabbed her handkerchief to his lips. It came away stained crimson. "Who did this to you?"

"We were worried. We saw you in the square," I said.

"Then you know!" Wilhelm blurted.

"Know what?"

"The Ammeister was stripped of his powers. He's in prison. Kaspar and his accomplices are in charge of the council now. They're governing Strasbourg, heaven help us!"

I pointed to his wounds. "Did Kaspar do this to you?"

"His friends beat me up. They're wild beasts," Wilhelm said. He gave a lopsided smile. "They're also nursing a few bruises themselves."

Vera and Elena exchanged amused glances.

"I'm older than all of you, but the foolish pride of men still amazes me," Vera said.

"Never mind that," Wilhelm said. "Why were the two of you in the town square instead of at work here, as you're supposed to be?"

"I wanted to go for a walk, Papa," Elena said. "I've been working so hard. I needed some fresh air."

He smiled reluctantly. But when I told him that the plague had arrived in our city, his expression became grim.

"Sweet Jesus," he cried. "We're in for terrible times!"

"There is something even more serious that I have to tell you, master."

"What could be more serious than the pestilence?"

And so I told him—about Kaspar poisoning the well and accusing the Jews of our city of the crime. I also told him about how I became an *ibbur* by the grace of the Almighty.

Wilhelm struggled to his feet. "Do you take me for a fool to tell me such a tale?" he roared.

"It's true, Papa! It's true!" Elena cried. "He is Natan and not Hans."

Her father sank to the bench once again. He looked me over from head to toe. "Could such a preposterous tale be true?" he muttered to himself. "It would explain why he acts so differently—forgetting everything about our trade, not eating our food, constantly washing his hands."

He looked at me again and I met his gaze.

"If you're Natan, son of Simon the Jew, tell me how much money I gave you when you brought your father's merchandise to me after he was set upon."

"You were very generous, master. You paid me with a gold coin. You also told me that you found my father to be an honest man, and that you held him in high regard. You sent him your wishes for his full recovery."

Amazement was written on Wilhelm's face.

"Only the Jew's son would know such details," he said to himself. "I feel that Hans must be Natan, but how can I be sure?"

"Because *I* am sure, Papa," Elena said. "Natan is telling you the truth. Despite his appearance, he is definitely not Hans. I know this with certainty."

"How can you?"

Elena took a deep breath and straightened her spine. "Because Natan and I loved . . . I mean, Natan and I *love* each other."

Although she'd corrected herself, her words were nevertheless a stab in my heart.

She dropped to her knees at her father's feet and put her head on his lap. "I'm sorry that I didn't tell you before, Papa, but I was worried you'd disapprove."

Wilhelm turned pale and slumped against the wall. "It's not my disapproval you need to worry about, girl. If the authorities discover your relationship, it's the stockades for you both—or even worse!" He turned to me angrily. "If you love her as you claim you do, how could you expose her to such danger?"

"Your daughter likes to have her way, master. She won't listen to me. She'll do what she likes."

Wilhelm looked stunned, and then slowly he began to rumble with laughter. "Now I believe you! You know my Elena well!"

Elena kissed his cheek and exclaimed, "I knew you would understand, Papa."

He patted her hand. "Now don't think that I'm not angry with you both." He sighed in resignation. "What can I do to help?"

"My people are innocent of poisoning the well, Master Wilhelm. I must save them somehow."

"The sooner your people leave Strasbourg, the better it will be for them. With Kaspar and his henchmen in power, the Jews will no longer be protected in our city. We must warn your parents and other members of your community of the danger."

"My father won't listen to anything I say." I felt so ashamed that I hung my head. "My mother told me that he's furious if she even mentions my name."

"You must convince him somehow. I'll go with you to see them." When he tried to stand, he fell back to the bench with a groan.

"You must rest, Papa!" Elena cried.

"Elena is right, master. You're battered and hurt. I'll go to my family by myself tomorrow and warn them of the danger. You'll come with me when your bruises are healed."

After much argument, he agreed to my proposition. I helped him to his bedchamber and left him to Vera's ministrations, groaning and complaining of the poultices she laid upon him.

I bade Elena good night. Her smile was so fair that I forgot myself for a moment and drew her close to my heart. I bent my head toward her lips, but when I heard her intake of breath, I turned on my heel and stalked out of the house.

The next morning, I walked at a brisk pace to Judenstrasse. I wanted to arrive home while my papa was out on his route. I prayed to the Almighty to soften my father's manner toward me. My heart beat in anticipation of seeing my mother and Shmuli, but I missed my father so much.

Suddenly, the clouds of time rolled away.

I'm at our Shabbos table with my family. Papa is at the head, dishing out the cholent that Mama has cooked. Mama is sitting across from him, smiling. The flickering candles in the center of the table cast shadows upon our faces.

"I'm hungry!" my brother cries.

Mama hands him a slice of our Sabbath bread.

"Eat, my little one! Eat!" she urges.

Papa turns to me.

"And you, my son, how did you spend your day?"

How I wished for life to be the same as before, but I knew it was not to be. I told myself that I had to be strong and think only of ways to save my people. Fear filled my heart, but I thought of Mama, Papa and Shmuli and realized that I couldn't—wouldn't—give up until my last breath.

I was so engrossed in my thoughts that I barely noticed the bright red crosses on the front doors of several of the houses I passed. The crosses, I knew, marked the places where victims of the plague and their families were quarantined. Curiously, there were no quarantine houses on Judenstrasse.

Finally, I arrived at what had once been my home. When I hammered on our front door, it flew open revealing Shmuli in the doorway with his thumb in his mouth. He stared at me mutely. I smiled at him, but he gazed back with a serious face.

"Get Mama for me." I pulled his thumb out of his mouth. "Stop it! You're eight years old. Only babies suck their thumbs."

"Who are you?" he asked, looking at me in a suspicious manner.

I didn't know how to reply. Should I say, "I'm your brother in a brand-new body"? Or should I answer, "I'm Hans, the journeyman draper"? Fortunately, our mother appeared in the doorway behind him, saving me from having to respond.

As Mama embraced me, Shmuli's eyes grew rounder. She grabbed his sleeve and drew him into our circle.

"The Almighty has sent the soul of your brother into the body of Hans," she said, pointing at me.

"Why would he do that?" Shmuli asked. He put his thumb back into his mouth and began to suck it noisily.

Mama pulled it out. "He's been sucking his thumb a lot more since you've been gone."

I pulled Shmuli closer. "The Almighty sent my soul into Hans because he wants me to save our people," I explained.

"We don't question God's reasons," Mama said. "Just be grateful that your brother is still with us."

Shmuli shrugged his shoulders and kept on peering at me furtively. But I noticed that he no longer pulled away from my embrace.

"Have a seat, my son, and stay a while. Your father won't be home for several hours." Her expression clouded. "I don't know what to do with him. He won't listen to anything I say about you."

"I can't stay, Mama. I wish I could spend more time with you and Shmuli, but I still have to warn our friends. Please tell Papa that Ammeister Schwarber and the master tradesmen are no longer in charge. Kaspar and his cronies are running the city."

"This means grief and hard times for us!" she cried.

"You're right. That's why Papa must make sure that all our friends and neighbors know. I'll speak to Rabbi Weltner myself. He must also know that the Ammeister has been stripped of his powers and was thrown into prison."

"Heaven help us! Peter Schwarber was the one who protected us. Although he charged a high price for his guardianship, he still kept us safe."

"You must leave our city as soon as possible," I urged. "There's no longer a place for Jews like us in Strasbourg."

"But where can we go? We've lived here for more generations than I can remember. What will happen to us?" She wiped her tears with the back of her hand and nodded to Shmuli, who was building a castle with wooden blocks in a corner of the room. "To him?"

I shrugged my shoulders helplessly. "I wish I could tell you, Mama. All I know is that the sooner our people leave Strasbourg, the safer it'll be for them."

The streets were already filled with frantic people as I made my way home. The news of the Great Pestilence was spreading quickly through our city. The roads were clogged with carts pulled by mules or their owners. They were filled to overflowing with the personal belongings of those trying to escape from Strasbourg. In some, children perched on wooden benches in the back. I walked along beside them.

Poor wretches! I said to myself. Where can they go? The plague will follow them everywhere. Nowhere is safe.

At the edge of town, the carts joined a longer procession heading down a dirt road. Sons and daughters supported aged parents. Fathers carried young children on their shoulders, while their older siblings ran around at the edge of the crowd. In one cart lay a pregnant woman, her hands clutching her swollen belly. A life will enter this world as others depart it, I thought.

A little girl, abandoned by her parents, stood in the middle of the road, weeping. "Mama, Papa," she wailed, "where are you?" Everyone simply walked around her.

Knights and their squires were leading horses burdened with armor and weaponry. Ladies in litters reclined with kerchiefs pressed to their noses as their attendants bumped them along. A holy man was crossing himself every few steps. The crowd was strangely quiet. No one turned around to look back at Strasbourg, their home. Everyone trudged on and on.

I retraced my steps to Wilhelm's workshop. When I drew close, I stopped at the back of a large crowd. Excited townspeople had surrounded a peddler and were eagerly buying his wares.

"What's he selling?" I asked the man next to me.

"Amulets made of dried toads."

"My amulets will protect you against the Great Pestilence," the peddler said. "I guarantee it."

"I'll buy one," said my neighbor, handing over his coins.

"I want one too!" announced a toothless old woman behind me.

Soon, the grinning peddler had filled up the money pouch hanging from his neck.

I passed on. A few steps away, a pilgrim was selling amulets made from the ground-up bones of a saint. I didn't even bother to stop.

When I reached Wilhelm's shop, I realized that I had forgotten to take my key with me. I knocked on the door and it flew open immediately. Elena threw herself into my arms.

"Thank God you're home!" she cried. "Papa is sick!"

ELENA'S STORY

CHAPTER 17

I was sitting by the window of our shop waiting for customers, but none came. Most people stayed at home, hiding from the pestilence. Others spent their days and nights in public houses, drinking, singing and carousing as if the end of the world was upon us. Perhaps it was.

Vera had gone to visit her sister and Natan was at Rabbi Weltner's house. Papa was resting in his room, still recovering from the aches and pains of the beating he had received at Kaspar's hands. I leaned back in my seat and closed my eyes, luxuriating in the silence. Immediately, all kinds of thoughts crowded unbidden into my head.

My Natan, strong and beautiful, is sitting beside me at the kitchen table. It's dark, the only source of light the moonbeams sneaking through the high window. They cast deep shadows on his cheekbones. He lifts my hand and kisses my palm. Shivers run down my spine.

"You're cold," he says, and pulls me closer.

He lowers his head and our lips meet.

"I love you," he whispers.

"I love you too," I tell him.

Suddenly, his shape shifts and he becomes Hans, with lanky hair and a greasy face. I push him away, revolted.

"Who are you?" I ask. "Where is my Natan?"

"Don't you know? I'm—"

Before I could hear his answer, a noise transported me back to reality. Papa was standing in the doorway, a tumbler of ale in his hand. His face was red and droplets of sweat dotted his brow.

"You should be in bed!" I scolded.

"I was thirsty. I came down to get some ale."

"Why didn't you call me? I'd have brought it upstairs. You're flushed." I put my hand over his brow as I would have done for a child. He was burning up. Fear squeezed my heart. "You're feverish, Papa!"

He laughed. "It's nothing. I must be coming down with the ague."

"Let me help you back to bed and then I'll bathe

your forehead to cool you down."

"You stay here. I'll go upstairs by myself. I don't need help."

He started off, but then staggered and would have fallen if I hadn't sprung up to support him. He leaned on me heavily, his arm around my neck, each step up the staircase a test of both our wills. I had to all but drag him up the steps. When we finally got to his bed-chamber, he fell onto his pallet, breathing heavily with his eyes screwed shut.

I pulled a blanket over him and mopped his brow. It was then that I noticed the large red boil on his neck. As I lifted him to put a pillow beneath his head, his eyes fluttered open.

"Go away!" he groaned. "Don't come close to me!"

I ran to the kitchen and prepared a cold compress. Please, God, don't let it be the Black Death, I kept repeating to myself as I made my way back upstairs.

The boil on Papa's neck was now the size of a baby's head and had turned black. He was breathing heavily, and suddenly he began to retch. I rolled him over to his side and held a bowl for him. It was soon filled with vomit mixed with blood. I didn't know what to do. I didn't want to leave him alone, but I had to go to fetch a surgeon. Everybody knew that bloodletting worked miracles.

Just then, there was a loud banging on our front door. I ran downstairs to open it. It was Natan. I threw myself into his arms.

"Thank God you're home!" I cried. "Papa is sick!"

He accompanied me to my father's room. I could see how affected he was by the way the color drained from his face.

"He looks terrible," he whispered.

"You must get the surgeon," I said. "He'll balance Papa's humors and restore his health."

He shot me a pitying glance but said, "I'll go right away."

Dark stains had bloomed under the skin of Papa's arms and legs by the time Natan and the surgeon appeared. The surgeon stood in the doorway, holding a scented handkerchief under his nose with one hand and a pail full of leeches in the other. Natan took a quick look at them squirming in the pail before saying he would leave to scrounge for food.

Once we were alone, the surgeon moved to Papa's bed. "I'm sorry to tell you, mistress, that the plague has arrived in your home," he announced portentously.

"I can see that. But please, master, what can you do to help my father?"

"Bloodletting will reduce the hotness of his blood. It may help in this case."

He ordered me to open Papa's shirt, then he pulled the squirming leeches out of the pail and placed the nightmarish creatures on his chest. Papa moaned but seemed otherwise unaware of what was being done to him. I screwed my eyes shut.

Once the leeches had done their work and were safely back in the pail, the surgeon took a long, sharp knife out of a sling by his side. He wiped it on his dirty apron and quickly lanced the boil on Papa's neck. The sickening stench of rotten eggs permeated the chamber and made my stomach heave.

I headed toward the window.

"Don't open it," the surgeon said. "You don't want fresh air on your father. In his weak condition, it might kill him."

I went to get a handkerchief instead and held it over my nose to stop myself from giving up my dinner in a most undignified manner.

Papa still seemed unaware of his surroundings. He tossed and turned and thrashed his arms and legs.

"He doesn't seem to be any better," I ventured to say as I counted silver coins into the surgeon's palm.

"It'll take time. You must be patient," he said. "Keep him comfortable. There's nothing more to be done for now." He turned in the doorway and added, "I regret to tell you, mistress, that I must place this dwelling under quarantine. Nobody goes in or out. I'll notify city authorities."

I nodded and walked him downstairs. With a bow and a flourish of his hat, he was gone. As soon as he'd disappeared, I pushed a stout chair to the front door and slid its tall back under the handle. Nobody would be able to enter the house from the outside. I also walked around the main floor and made sure all the windows were locked.

I had just finished my inspection when some loud banging from the street led me back to the front entrance.

"Open the door! It's me, Natan. I've brought us food."

"I can't! We're under quarantine. The red cross will be painted on our door very soon. It's dangerous for you to come in."

"Don't be silly, Elena. I'm not scared of the sickness."

"Then you're a fool! Leave the food in front of the door and get as far away from this house as you can."

I turned a deaf ear to his appeals until he finally gave up and left. Only then did I open the door and retrieve a basket filled with dark bread and a pitcher of ale. I put some of the bread on a plate, poured the ale into a tankard and carried them upstairs. I couldn't stir my father enough to make him eat, but I did wet his lips with the ale. Then I went back downstairs and ate my own meal. It tasted like sawdust in my mouth.

The next day, Papa remained insensible. I tried to keep him as comfortable as I could by changing his bedding, giving him a dry shirt and wiping his brow and hands with cold water. Despite my ministrations, more boils appeared under his arms and in his groin area. I couldn't think of anything else to do except to fall on my knees and beg God for his mercy. I prayed on my father's behalf to the Lord Jesus and his mother, but they weren't listening to me. Papa remained in torment.

"Get better, Papa. Get better. I couldn't bear to lose you!" I pleaded.

He too remained deaf to my words.

What if you catch the pestilence from him? a little voice whispered in my ear. You should leave while you still can, before you get sick too! There is nothing more you can do for him.

I fell on my knees once again and prayed until I ran out of words. I begged our Lord to give me the strength to do the right thing.

I must have fallen asleep with my head on Papa's chest, for a sudden noise startled me back to wakefulness. Somebody was throwing stones at the window high up on the wall of Papa's bedchamber.

I pushed a bench below the window and climbed on top of it to see outside. I flung open the shutters and felt the cold air rushing into the chamber. Natan and Vera were in the street, waving to me. There was a basket on the snowy ground beside their feet.

"How is your dear papa faring?" Vera asked. She began to weep.

"He isn't well. He's still unconscious. Nobody is allowed to come into the house or to leave it."

Vera crossed herself. "May the good Lord take care of him."

"I've brought you food," Natan said.

"I'm not hungry and Papa is too sick."

"You must eat to keep up your strength. Come to the door. I'll give it to you."

"No, I don't want to get so close to you. My miasma—"

"Go downstairs and open the door," Natan said in a firm voice.

"I won't. I don't want you to catch the sickness."

"You don't have to worry about that. I've been helping Rabbi Weltner nurse the sick in Judenstrasse. It's the only place where his aid is welcome." He smiled broadly. "As you can see, I'm still in good health."

"I must bid you good-bye first, young mistress, for I must return to my sister's," Vera interjected. "I won't see you for a while. My sister has been infected by this terrible plague, and it's my duty to nurse her."

"I pray to God that you'll succeed."

"And I you, mistress."

I shut the window and descended the staircase. Natan was waiting for me in front of the door, the basket clasped in his hand. After looking down the street both ways to make sure that nobody was observing him, he pushed me gently aside and mounted the steps, two at a time, to Papa's bedchamber.

"You shouldn't be here, Natan," I said wearily. "The Great Pestilence might carry you away."

He grasped my hand. "I'm not frightened, my love. My fate is in Hashem's hands."

He crossed to the bowl of water I kept on the table, dipped a cloth and wiped Papa's forehead with it. He smiled at my father with such sweetness that it broke my heart. But Papa was too feverish to recognize him.

"Poor devil. He is burning up," he said as he pushed Papa's damp hair off his brow.

Suddenly, my stomach growled loudly.

He grinned. "You're hungrier than you know. Come, let us make you a meal."

I began to protest, but he waved my objections aside.

"Elena, you must eat and keep up your strength," he repeated.

We went outside to the kitchen and I unpacked the basket. Food was scarce nowadays, so he had filled it with whatever goodies he could find. There were nuts, ale, bread again and even two roasted partridge eggs carefully wrapped in a clean rag. At the sight of them, I found, to my surprise, that I was famished.

"There's enough here for both of us," I said.

"I can't stay. Rabbi Weltner is expecting me."

"Be careful."

"Hashem will look after me. He has already proven that," he said, smiling. "I'll try to bring you more food tomorrow."

Once he was gone, I poured some ale into a cup and picked up a knife, intending to cut myself a slice of bread. I noticed that my fingers were stained with Papa's blood, and that there was grime under my nails. I remembered how Natan always washed his hands before he ate. Suddenly, it didn't seem right to eat with such dirty hands, so I washed mine too. Then I had my meal, my mind lost in the gentleness of his expression and the kindness of his smile.

CHAPTER 18

Even with the shutters closed, I could hear the corpse removers on the street calling, "Bring out your dead! Bring out your dead!" When I opened the shutters and looked out the window, I could see the street. Drapers' Row was clear of the throngs that usually filled it, for Strasbourg was on its way to becoming a ghost town. There was no hawker offering vegetables, and the urchins promising the tastiest pies in the world had disappeared. The only people in the street had sweet-smelling herbs pressed to their noses and their belongings strapped to their backs. All of them seemed to be heading toward the edge of the city.

Where do you think you're hurrying to? I wanted to shout. Everywhere is the same! The plague has no favorites. Don't you know that it's the end of the world? There is nowhere to go! In the end, it will come for us all.

But then I wondered if I was wrong. Maybe they would find a place the plague had forgotten. Maybe I could find it too if I went with them. I looked at my father, insensible to the world around him. I smelled the stench of death surrounding him and knew I could do nothing more for him. And yet . . .

I fell to my knees and begged the Lord to give me the strength to be a good daughter.

The scene on our street was macabre. A red cross had been smeared on the majority of houses, and the bodies of deceased family members covered the front steps, waiting to be picked up by the death cart. In the building across from ours, I saw a body pushed out a second-story window to fall on top of the pile of corpses that filled the two-wheeled cart like so many rag dolls.

Long gone were the funeral processions with members of the mourning family veiled in black, their numbers supplemented by the professional mourners they had hired to follow the bier to the cemetery. The torchbearers, the candles and the guild flags had also disappeared. At the most, one mourner walked behind the death cart to express his grief.

Papa was getting worse and I was growing more desperate. When Natan paid his daily visit to bring us food, I gave him my last gold coin and asked him to go to the apothecary's shop and purchase a treacle made of roasted viper's flesh. But even that potent medicine didn't help my father.

I was spending most of my days on my knees begging the Lord to save my father's life. I was so absorbed in my thoughts that at first I didn't even hear the banging downstairs. When it finally penetrated my awareness, I ignored it. Who would be foolish enough to come to a house with a red cross smeared on its front door? But the banging wouldn't stop, so I decided to see who it was. I opened the door a crack and there she was, the last person I expected to see— Natan's mother.

"Mistress, why are you here? You must go away. My father is sick with the pestilence!"

"I know. Natan told me. I've come to help." She lifted the basket hanging from her arm. It was filled with all manner of jars and plants. "Please let me come inside. I've brought potions to help your father."

"I can't do that, dear lady. You might catch his illness and die!"

She smiled sweetly. "Don't worry about me. The Master of the Universe will take care of me, just as he took care of my Natan."

She pushed gently on the door and I stepped back. It swung open.

"I'm skilled at mixing healing potions. I learned the art at my mother's knee, as she learned it from her mother. I speak very little of this talent outside of our community, for I don't wish to be burned at the stake as a witch. But I put my fears to rest when I heard about your father's illness. We owe too much to you for your loyalty and friendship to Natan." She dismissed my objections with a wave of her hand. "Take me to your papa's bedchamber, please."

She stood by my father's bed for a long time without touching him. She stared at the huge black boils and the purple stains blooming under his skin. "Poor soul," she whispered. "He might be too far gone for my ministrations, but let me try." She looked at me pityingly. "I must tell you, I hold out little hope for him."

She glanced around the chamber and walked over to the bowl I had filled with water. There was a bar of soap next to it. I needed both the water and the soap to wash my father's face.

"I'd like clean water, please."

"But, mistress, there is nothing wrong with the water here. I just used it on my papa's face and hands."

"That's why I need clean water."

I shrugged my shoulders. I guessed she knew what she was doing, and even if not, I had nothing to lose. I ran downstairs and returned with a fresh bowl filled with water. She scrubbed her hands with the soap and poured water over them several times. I handed her Papa's towel, but she asked me to give her a clean cloth to dry her hands.

Next, she mixed together powders from the jars in her basket and dissolved them in Papa's ale. Her draft smelled of rosemary. I put my arm under Papa's shoulders and lifted his head so that she could pour her potion into his throat. He coughed a little but swallowed it.

Once we were finished, I covered my father with his blanket once again. His eyes remained shut.

"It's in God's hands now," she said. "We've done all we can. I hope he'll recover, for he is a good man, kind to everybody." She smiled at me. "As are you."

Her gaze swept around the room, taking in my father's snowy blanket, his clean hands and face, and the small blue vase with bulrushes on the scrubbed table in the center of the chamber.

"You're a good daughter, Elena," she said.

"And you're even a better friend. Thank thee, mistress."

"I can never forget the kindness you've shown my Natan." She sighed. "He wants us to leave Strasbourg, you know."

"And he's right to say it. With Kaspar and his friends in power, there is nobody to protect Jews like you any longer."

"I don't understand why people blame us for the Great Pestilence. Surely they must see that Kaspar is lying!

After all, many of us have died from the sickness as well. And nobody would wish such a scourge upon the world."

She returned to the table and scrubbed her hands before packing her basket with her potions and preparing to leave.

"Peter Schwarber is our only hope," she said finally. "He's an honorable man, and he won't desert us."

"But how can the Ammeister help you when he's in prison?"

"He'll think of a way." Her face darkened. "I have to hold firmly to this belief because my husband refuses to leave Strasbourg."

As we descended the staircase and I continued to express my gratitude for her kindness, I couldn't help saying, "Mistress, I noticed that you washed your hands before you touched my father and also after you finished treating him. Natan says that washing hands is a part of your religion. He washes his hands before every meal."

"Oh yes, Jews must wash their hands upon waking each morn and also before eating their bread. We greet our Sabbath not only with clean souls but also with clean bodies. After all, the body is the vessel given to us by our Lord." She smiled. "Once you're clean, there is no going back."

After she left, I returned to my papa's chamber. It smelled of rosemary. His poor, tortured belly wasn't able to tolerate the medicine Natan's mother had given him.

CHAPTER 19

Papa's breathing was becoming more and more tortured with every passing moment. Four days after he became ill, he stopped breathing for such a long time that I thought he had been gathered to Jesus. But after a few horrific moments, he began again. I knew it was time to ask our priest to administer last rites and absolve my papa of his sins, and I also knew I couldn't wait to ask Natan to fetch Father Albrecht when he brought me food. I disliked Father Albrecht's pursed lips and his gnarled and grimy hands, which were always clasped in showy piety, but he was a man of God and Papa needed him. So I kissed my father's burning cheek and set out on my mission.

I was afraid to leave by the front door with its red cross, a declaration to all that our house was under quarantine. But I was puzzled for a moment, for the front door was the only one leading directly to the street. Then I thought of the garden behind the house and the gate where Natan and I used to meet in happier times. That would let me out into the laneway, unseen by my neighbors' prying eyes. Before I had a chance to lose my nerve, I ran across the yard and was gone.

The streets were eerily silent and almost empty except for the corpse carriers. More bodies were lying in front of houses and in the street. I looked away when I saw a rat gnawing on the arm of a dead woman with pale hair. At the corner, ragged urchins were cutting chunks of flesh from the body of a dead mule.

As soon as I entered the cathedral, my gaze was drawn up to the high roof straining to meet the heavens and my heart was filled with joy. But as the stench of death permeated my senses, reality intruded.

The church was empty except for a black-robed figure slumped over in the front pew.

"Father Albrecht?" I called out as I approached. "Please, Father, I need your help."

No answer. I hesitated but then went closer. The priest was barely recognizable with his grotesquely swollen face, humongous black boils on his neck and purple stains under his skin. There was nothing I could do except rush out of the church as if a thousand devils were chasing me. In a way, they were.

I ran for home, blinded by tears until I caught the strains of a faraway song:

Eternal rest give unto the dead, O Lord,
And let perpetual light shine upon them.
Eternal rest give unto them, O Lord,
And let perpetual light shine upon them.

Lord, have mercy on us.
Christ, have mercy on us.
Lord, have mercy on us.

I ran toward the music. As I rounded a corner, my path was blocked by a long line of monks marching down the icy road. Their black-and-white robes identified them as Dominicans whose monastery was on a hill outside Strasbourg. The prior was at the head of the procession carrying a wooden box. I knew that it must hold the remains of a saint. Several of the monks were bent under the weight of large wooden crosses. They were all chanting the prayer for the dead. The few stragglers in the street fell to their knees and crossed themselves as the monks passed. I followed their example and knelt there on the cold ground, oblivious to the tears streaming down my cheeks.

An aged monk at the very end of the procession stopped in front of me. The rest of his group kept on moving, leaving him behind.

"Can I help you, my child?" He reached out and helped me off the ground.

"My father is dying. I must find a priest for him. I want my papa to go to heaven."

"If your father is a good man, the Lord Jesus will gather him under his wings," he said in a kindly voice.

I wept even harder. "My papa is a churchgoing man. He would want a priest to attend to him as the end approaches."

"I'm just a humble monk, but I'll come with you and see what I can do."

I fell to my knees again and kissed the hem of his robe. "May the Lord bless you for your kindness!"

"Don't be foolish, child. I'm only doing my duty." He smiled a little. "I'm Brother Jurian."

He followed me home. Papa was still alive—but barely. Brother Jurian made the sign of the cross on his forehead and sprinkled his body with holy water. He anointed him with oil and blessed him, then he absolved him of his sins. When he finished, he took his leave.

Once again, I was alone with my papa. I sat down beside him and said good-bye. How I wished that Natan was with me to share my pain! His face appeared in front of my eyes—at first as he used to be, and then as he became. I would have welcomed his presence either way, but it was not to be. So I took my father's hand into my own and began to talk to him. I reminded him of the jolly time we'd shared when he took me for my first mule ride when I was a babe. I told him of my joy when he bought me my favorite straw doll on my name day. I spoke of his patience when he taught me how to help him in our shop. I said he'd never raised his voice in anger, not even once. By the time I finished speaking, Papa's face was waxen and still. I closed his eyes and blessed him and kissed him good-bye.

I climbed to the window and opened it a crack, then settled down to wait. The cold air caused chilblains on my hands. Finally, I heard the death cart coming.

"Bring out your dead! Bring out your dead!" the corpse bearers shouted.

I leaned out the window. "My father has passed on to a better place," I called.

The cart stopped below the window.

"Bring him out," said one of the corpse bearers.

"I'm all alone. I don't have the strength."

He shrugged. "Push him through the window."

I looked at my papa, so peaceful in his eternal sleep. "I'm too weak to do that. You'll have to come upstairs to help me."

He cursed in a most foul way, but he headed toward our door nonetheless. His partner followed him. I ran downstairs to let them in.

The men reeked of spirits and of death, but I was grateful to them all the same. I led them to my papa's bed. They grabbed him by the neck and feet, and set off to carry him downstairs.

"Wait!" I cried. "He must have a burial shroud."

The first man looked at me as if I had lost my senses, but then he shrugged his shoulders.

"Let's roll him in his blanket," he said.

While we were talking, the younger man dumped the bulrushes from the blue vase onto the table and dropped the vase into a large pouch at his waist. He looked at me with challenge in his eyes, but I held my peace.

It seemed a sin to allow them to touch my father, but what could I do? They carried him down the stairs to the street. I followed them outside and tried not to look as they threw him on the mountain of corpses, but I still saw what they were doing.

I trailed the cart down the street, the only mourner in sight. When we came to the cemetery behind the cathedral, the men kept going.

"Hey, stop!" I cried. "The cemetery is over there."

"The cemetery is full. We're taking him to the pit outside the city walls," the older man said over his shoulder.

I had no choice but to follow meekly behind them.

At the gate to the city, the man turned around again. "You can't come any farther. You must stay here."

"Why?"

"It's the law. Nobody is allowed to go near the pit."

"Nobody except us," his friend added.

They both began to guffaw loudly, as if enjoying the most amusing of jests.

I stood and watched them take my papa away. Then I turned around and made my way home.

CHAPTER 20

I t was lonely in my home without my papa. I sat all by myself, remembering the good times he and I had—Papa feeding the hearth with logs and telling me scary stories that made me seek the safety of his arms; Papa singing loudly and clapping his hands as I danced around the maypole with other maids; and Papa telling me how proud he was of me and how much he loved me, over and over again. Most of all, I missed his laughter. The house was a dreary place without him.

A sudden noise made me jump, but it was just a little mouse scurrying across the rushes on the floor. I wished for the comfort of Vera's embrace, but she still hadn't returned from her sister's house. At least I could go and see Natan now, and help him and Rabbi Weltner nurse the Jewish plague victims.

As I set out for Judenstrasse, I was startled to realize that whenever I thought of Natan, it was the homely face of Hans that swam before my eyes and not the handsome countenance of the boy I had loved and lost.

I lined up behind an old Jewish man waiting to be allowed to enter the Street of the Jews by the sentries guarding the gate. One of the watchmen walked up to the man and spat in his face. He wiped his cheek with the back of his hand, but he didn't object. He kept his eyes fixed on the ground.

"Tell me, you Jewish devil, what were you up to today? How many Christians did you poison in our fair town?"

"I had some business to attend to, master, but I did nothing wrong," the old man muttered. "Please, master, I just want to go home."

"How *much* do you want to go home?" the older sentry asked.

The man stared at him for a long moment until comprehension finally flooded his face. I saw the quick exchange of a coin from the old man's palm into the guard's paw. The guard stepped aside and the old man scurried past, moving as fast as his bent legs would allow.

I reached into the pouch hanging around my neck and extracted one of the few coins I had left. I held it out toward the younger sentry, who snatched it from my hand. His gaze traveled down my body.

"Why is a fine maid like you heading to Judenstrasse?" he slurred.

His breath reeked so strongly of spirits that I had to force myself not to turn my head away. I couldn't think of a reply, so I batted my eyes flirtatiously to distract him. He came even closer and grabbed my wrist.

"Well, then, it seems that you're up for some fun and games. You won't regret it!"

I pushed him away playfully. "I wish I could stay, but Kaspar, the new Ammeister, is a special friend of mine . . . if you know what I mean. He would be upset if I stayed too long in Judenstrasse."

He dropped my hand as if it belonged to a leper.

"You're Kaspar's wench? Why didn't you say so?" he muttered, stepping out of my way.

I forced myself to stroll down the street as if I didn't have a care in the world. Only when out of sight did I break into a run as if the devil himself were chasing me.

Like my own street, Judenstrasse was devoid of life and all the shops were shuttered. I saw some houses with red crosses painted on their doors, but there were far fewer of these plague houses than on my own street.

I passed three little boys with long sidelocks playing marbles on the frozen cobblestones. They reminded me of Natan's brother, Shmuli.

Eventually, I arrived at Rabbi Weltner's house behind the synagogue. I knocked on the front door. It opened a crack and an old woman with a cast in her eye stuck out her head.

"What you want?"

"I'm here to see Hans, the journeyman draper. I heard that he is staying with you."

"Maybe he is, maybe he isn't," she muttered. "Who are you?"

"I'm—"

Before I could finish, the door opened wider and Natan appeared. I pushed the woman aside and ran into his arms. For an instant, his homely face was beautiful in my eyes. The woman started toward me.

"It's all right, Agnes," he said. "She's a friend of mine."

With curses under her breath, the woman shut the front door and disappeared.

"Don't mind her," Natan said. "She seems rough, but her heart is in the right place. She is most loyal to Rabbi Weltner." His face darkened. "But why are you here? Your father . . . ?"

"I had nowhere else to go." I began to sob. "My papa has joined the angels. I came to help you nurse the sick."

"I'm so sorry for your loss. Wilhelm was such a kind man. A good man." His voice broke. "I will miss him too." He rubbed his eyes. "I'm certain the rabbi will welcome you with open arms once you explain your situation to him." He squeezed my fingers reassuringly.

It felt so safe being with him that I moved even closer and put my head on his shoulder. He leaned back to look into my eyes.

"Why, Elena—"

Suddenly, there was a loud knock. I stepped away from him in haste.

"A day for unexpected arrivals," he said, opening the door.

A tall man, his features obscured by the hood of his cloak, stood on the threshold. He pushed his hood back to reveal his face—it was Peter Schwarber. His eyes scanned the street behind him and he breathed a sigh of relief when he saw that nobody else was in sight. Despite being a big man, he seemed somehow diminished. Was it the pallor of his complexion? The nervous twitch of his lips? I couldn't tell, but I knew for sure that I wasn't looking at the same person I had seen at the town hall.

Natan bowed low in front of him and I bobbed a deep curtsy.

"Welcome, Ammeister," he said. "What can I do for you?"

"I must see Rabbi Weltner," he replied, stepping into the house.

NATAN'S STORY

CHAPTER 21

I could still feel her breath fanning my neck as I led Peter Schwarber to Rabbi Weltner's door and knocked.

"Come in!"

I ushered the Ammeister into the room and motioned for Elena to follow. The rabbi was sitting at the table, rolls of parchment piled up in front of him. When he saw Schwarber, he stood up and extended his hand.

"Ammeister, what a welcome surprise! I was told you were in prison. I'm glad to see you a free man."

"Ammeister no longer," Schwarber said sadly, sitting down across from the rabbi. "I was released from jail this morning."

Elena and I sat down beside him. The rabbi kept on staring at Schwarber thoughtfully and made no comment on Elena's presence. He filled four silver goblets with ale and gave them to us.

"How can I be of assistance to you, Ammeister?"

"I am the one who wants to be of assistance to you and your people, Rabbi," Schwarber said. He cleared his throat. "I've heard some terrible rumors. Kaspar and the remaining councilors are making plans against the Jews of Strasbourg." He sighed heavily. "They're planning to destroy you. To kill every last one of you."

A sudden intake of breath was the only sound in the room.

"Are you certain about this?" the rabbi asked.

"Yes, I am. They're planning to have you dig your own graves in your cemetery and then they'll bury you in them."

"T-that's . . . unbelievable," the rabbi stuttered.

Elena was crying and my own heart was hammering so loudly that I could barely hear Schwarber's response.

"I'm telling you the truth, Rabbi. I overheard Kaspar plotting with his friends. I couldn't live with myself if I allowed them to kill you."

He spoke calmly and forcefully, his fingers intertwined so tightly that his knuckles had turned white.

Rabbi Weltner wiped his forehead with a snowy handkerchief. "How can you help us?"

"I've a plan," Schwarber said. "Tell your neighbors that they're to go to the Jewish cemetery tomorrow morn when the sun rises. My men will accompany them, to convince Kaspar and his henchmen that you're in my power."

"That can be arranged," Rabbi Weltner said.

"I'll have horse-drawn carts waiting for the old and the sick at the cemetery. They'll be driven to the Black Forest. The rest of you can walk there. It's a long walk—it'll take you the best part of two days—but it can be done. By the time Kaspar realizes that you've left the cemetery, you'll be hidden in the forest."

The rabbi shook Schwarber's hand fiercely. "Thank you, Ammeister!"

Elena had stopped crying and was grinning from ear to ear. But something about Schwarber's demeanor disturbed me. The Ammeister's eyes kept shifting from the rabbi to Elena to me and then back to the rabbi, as if he was gauging our reactions to his story.

"What will we do in the forest?" I asked him.

"Ah! I wondered when you'd ask. I've hired guides to lead you through the woods. When you reach the other side, you should plan to travel to lands far away in the east and begin new lives."

"New lives? Nobody wants us!" I spluttered. "Why would they allow us to settle among them?"

"You worry too much," Schwarber said, waving off my concerns. "Everything will work out for you."

He stood and picked up his hat. "I must go now, for I have much to do. Tomorrow, when the sun begins her climb to the top of the sky, I'll return with my men. Spread the word among your friends and neighbors. By the time Kaspar and his councilors figure out what's happened, you'll be on your way to freedom in the Black Forest."

Rabbi Weltner grabbed Schwarber's hand and did something I'd never seen him do before—he bent low over it and kissed it.

"My dear Ammeister, how can we ever repay you?"

Schwarber's face turned red and a look of shame spread across his features. It was gone so quickly that I thought I had imagined it.

"No need to thank me," he said. "You've paid enough for my protection over the years. That's all I'm doing—protecting you."

Then, with a deep bow, he was gone.

"What a great man!" the rabbi cried. "May Hashem bless him!"

Elena fell to her knees. "Thank thee, Lord Jesus, for keeping Natan and his people safe!" she said.

"Let's knock on our neighbors' doors and ask them to spread the word," Rabbi Weltner suggested. He ran his fingers through his beard and turned to me. "Natan, you go with Elena to the houses on the right and I'll speak to the rest of our people. Unfortunately, several members of our community are fighting the plague and must be left behind."

I weighed my words carefully before speaking. "Are you certain we're doing the right thing? I don't trust Peter Schwarber."

His eyes opened wide. "Whyever not? Schwarber is a man of his word. He has always protected us in the past."

"He was just released from prison. Why would he risk losing his freedom again by helping us?"

"You worry too much, Natan," the rabbi said. "If we follow the Ammeister's plan, all will be well."

"I agree with Rabbi Weltner," Elena said. "My papa always said that Schwarber was an honorable man."

"I don't know. There was something about the way he was looking at us. What if he just wants to save his own skin by delivering us into Kaspar's hands?"

"He is our friend," the rabbi insisted. "He has our best interests at heart."

When we went to our neighbors' doors to warn them, relief greeted us at every turn. Not a single person doubted Schwarber's plan. I tried to convince myself that I was wrong. I told myself that here was my opportunity to save my people, to lead them through the Black Forest to freedom. Finally, I would be able to do what Hashem expected of me. But then I recalled Schwarber's unease, and all my doubts came galloping back.

My breath caught in my throat when I saw the dreaded red cross painted on Meyer the moneylender's dwelling, two doors away from my parents'. I began to breathe again only when I saw that their door didn't bear the same macabre decoration.

Shmuli answered my knock. His eyes became saucers at the sight of me and his thumb returned to his mouth.

"Call Mama to the door," I whispered.

I told my mother about Schwarber's plan.

"Thank God, we're saved!" she cried. She pushed me away and began to shut the door. "Go now, before your father sees you! He'd be furious if he knew that you'd been here!"

The door shut in my face before I could share my doubts about Schwarber.

"Time to go home," I told Elena. "I'll walk you back."

We'd barely reached the corner of Judenstrasse when we were pushed to the side of the street by a large group of half-naked men. We squashed ourselves against the front of a building. I put my arm around Elena and turned her face into my shoulder. I didn't want her to see the men thrashing themselves with leather whips with iron spikes. Blood was running down their faces and their bodies.

"Death to the Jews! Death to the poisoners of the wells!" they roared.

"They brought the Great Pestilence upon us! Kill them!" cried a man from the middle of the crowd, his eyes fierce in his bloodied face.

"We must go back and warn your family," Elena said.

"Let's stay close to the wall."

We linked hands and began to retrace our steps, but it was no use. The rabid horde blocked our way. Finally, we gave up and returned to Elena's home.

"Your parents and Shmuli will be fine as long as they stay indoors," she said, calming my fears while I lit a fire in the hearth.

We sat by the fire and talked until the logs became cinders and the chamber grew icy. I repeated my doubts about Schwarber to her, but she told me not to be foolish. I fell silent, but I couldn't still the niggling doubt in the pit of my stomach.

I was glad of the darkness surrounding us, for it hid my ugly face. I was too cowardly to share my feelings with her.

By the time I returned to the rabbi's house, the flagellants had left. The street was full of debris and broken furniture. Many residents of Judenstrasse were beaten up and injured. Fortunately, Rabbi Weltner and my family were not among them.

I had another dream that night:

> *I am all alone in the middle of a forest. I'm looking*
> *for something, but I can't remember what I've lost.*
> *A gigantic tree in my path bursts into flames. The*
> *heat is intense and the fire spreads to the trees around*
> *me, until I'm surrounded by flames. Suddenly, Hans*
> *appears in their midst. He is pale and trembling. Tears*
> *are running down his cheeks. He holds out his arms*
> *toward me in supplication.*
>
> *"I want to come home! I want to come home!"*
> *he cries.*

When I woke up, I was drenched to the skin and trembling with fear.

CHAPTER 22

Before dawn of that cold morn, the Jews of Strasbourg lined up in Judenstrasse, their belongings on their backs. I was among them. There must have been close to two thousand souls hemmed in by the buildings on both sides of the street. I noticed one of Master Wilhelm's costumers standing close by. I nodded to him.

"Hans, what are you doing here?" he asked.

The crowd carried him away before I could reply.

In the distance I spotted Shmuli, his hair burnished by the rising sun. He was holding on tightly to Mama's hand and rubbing his eyes groggily. Papa stood next to him, talking to his neighbors.

"Don't be angry with me. I had to come," said a voice behind my back. "I didn't want to leave you."

I turned around. It was Elena. I opened my arms wide and she fell into them. For an instant, the crowds receded and there were only two of us left in the entire world.

Reality soon intruded, however, with the arrival of Peter Schwarber. He was followed by a long line of guardsmen armed with knives and whips. They had surrounded us before my neighbors even realized what was happening. I drew Elena closer and looked around. There he was—Kaspar, lurking at the back of the crowd. His face was shaded by the hood of his cloak, but the rising sun illuminated his features for a short moment. It was long enough for me to see his red goatee and know I wasn't mistaken.

Kaspar and Schwarber were soon in deep conversation. Schwarber was talking vehemently, gesticulating with his arms. Finally, after nodding his assent, Kaspar moved away and tried to blend into the crowd. Only his great height allowed me to keep track of him.

"Kaspar is here," I told Elena.

"Where?"

I pointed him out.

"Why would Schwarber bring him along?"

"Our former Ammeister isn't what he claims to be. I suspect all he cares about is saving his own skin."

She shot me a worried look. "I fear you may be right."

Schwarber reached the front of the crowd and climbed on top of an upended cart. He began to address us.

"My friends," he cried, "today you will begin the rest of your lives—a life without prejudice and false accusations made against you. I will lead you to your cemetery at the edge of our town. From there, you will be guided to the Black Forest and helped to cross it safely. When you arrive on the other side, you will be free to travel to city-states located to the east. The inhabitants of these places await you with open arms." He paused. "Does anybody have any questions?"

A dark-haired, stocky man raised his hand.

"We're grateful for your help, Ammeister, but why did you bring the guardsmen with you?"

"Yes, why?" parroted several of his neighbors.

Schwarber smiled warmly, but I noticed that his good cheer didn't reach his eyes.

"You're an astute young man," he said. "I've brought my men with me to convince the new Ammeister that I'm driving you to your cemetery by force and getting you to dig your own graves. Little does Kaspar know that I'm taking you to your freedom."

His voice was so full of conviction and good cheer that I could see the hesitation drain out of the faces surrounding me. I had to stop him!

"Your evil plan won't work, Schwarber!" I said. "Kaspar knows of your scheme because you hatched it together. Both you and Kaspar are conspiring against the Jews of Strasbourg."

"Have you lost your senses, boy?" Rabbi Weltner whispered.

Schwarber turned toward me. "Why are you telling such lies?" he roared. He began to address the crowd again. "Remember, my friends, that these foolish accusations are coming from Hans, the journeyman draper." He pointed his finger at me. "Never forget that Hans is a Christian and not one of your people!"

Such fury invaded my body that it was an effort to speak coherently.

"I'm not the liar here. It's Schwarber who lies. He isn't telling you the truth. He conspired with Kaspar against you. He even brought the new Ammeister along with him," I said. "Kaspar is here, in the crowd among us!"

I turned toward the spot where I'd seen the butcher an instant before, but he was gone. My eyes scanned the crowd. The tall figure had disappeared.

"He's gone," I muttered. "But he was here moments ago."

"I saw him too," Elena confirmed.

"Did I not tell you that Hans is the most foul of liars?" Schwarber said. "So is his whore. Ignore them, for you have more important things on your mind. You must follow my instructions to save your lives!"

Several of my neighbors shot angry glances in my direction and slung their bundles over their shoulders, all ready to go.

"Master Schwarber, I've always found Hans to be an honest man," said the same dark-haired man as before. Only then did I recognize him. He was Fritz the bricklayer, the person I had failed to greet on our way home from the River Ill.

"If Hans is uneasy with your plan, so am I," he said. He hoisted his belongings and turned on his heel. "I'm going home."

"So am I," said his comrade.

"Me too," cried somebody else in the crowd.

At that instant, Kaspar walked out the front door of a house behind Schwarber. Immediately, all authority seeped from Schwarber's face and his body sagged.

With the arrival of the new Ammeister, more people turned around and started to make their way home.

"Stop!" Schwarber shouted, but they didn't heed him.

"Sentries, go!" Kaspar cried.

His henchmen unfurled their whips and began to beat the crowd of frightened Jews. One old man who fell was trampled by people fleeing for their lives. We were powerless against the brutality of the armed guards.

I knew there was a narrow lane behind the houses, leading away from the Street of the Jews. I had taken this path as a shortcut every time I'd visited Elena before my death. I put my arm around her waist now and pulled her toward the lane. Those nearby followed our example.

"Run!" I told her. "Run for your life!"

"Come with me!"

"I can't! I must remain with my family."

She stood there, looking at me, not moving.

I pushed her as hard as I dared. "Go! Go!"

She broke into a run but then stopped in her tracks and turned back around.

"I love you, Natan! I love you!" she cried before running away.

The armed brutes drove the rest of us to the Jewish cemetery beyond the city walls. If anybody stopped— even for an instant—a knife in the back was his reward. I tried to elbow my way closer to my family, but to no avail. I was mere flotsam carried along by a wave of desperate Jewish souls.

When we got to the cemetery, we saw that several huge wooden platforms had been built over the graves. Beside them were piles and piles of firewood. Our masters drove us up the platforms like cattle.

I managed to climb down from the platform I was on. When a guard tried to force me back up, I began to shout: "I'm not one of them! I'm not a Jew!" I pointed to my cloak. "See? I don't have the badge of the Jews. I'm here to assist you."

The man turned his attention from me and began to beat a hapless old lady bent over her cane. She was easier game.

"This'll teach you to plot against our city!" he roared at her.

The guards spread the firewood around the perimeter of each platform. If anybody resisted, he was stabbed.

Kaspar was everywhere—shouting orders and whipping terrified Jews. Schwarber was behind him, ready to fulfill his every whim. Finally, Kaspar lit the wood around the first platform. Schwarber lit the second and the third, until the fire spread to all the platforms. Soon, the sound of screams and the stench of roasting flesh filled the air.

Priests with crosses were running around the conflagration. "Repent! Repent!" they cried. "Accept Christ and you will be saved!" Some of the victims chose life and the baptismal font. I couldn't blame them. Other priests pried children out of the arms of their protesting parents and christened them against their will.

I began to search for my family. Time was running out. I found them on the platform closest to the cemetery gates, surrounded by fire and men with whips and knives. Everything seemed to be happening in slow motion, as if in a dream. I was standing outside my body, gazing at the horror in front of my eyes. Mama was lying facedown with the fire consuming her. The body of Rabbi Weltner was on the platform next to her. Papa was the only one standing tall. He was holding Shmuli in his embrace, protecting my brother's face with his arms. Papa's hair and beard were ablaze, and charred rags hung from his frame. I could see his lips moving. I knew that he was saying the *Shema*, the prayer every Jewish person says at the time of death.

"Help your brother, my son! Help him!" he cried when he spotted me.

His words jolted me back to reality. I held my arms out toward him. "Give him to me!"

He fought his way to the edge of the platform and threw Shmuli into my waiting arms. My brother's clothes were on fire.

"Papa, come!" I extended my hand. "I'll help you off the platform."

"I can't leave your mother," he said. "Good-bye, my son. Forgive me!"

At that moment, a guard ran up to us with his whip and felled my father to his knees. I ran through the cemetery gates with my brother while the man's back was to me. As soon as we were out of sight, I dropped Shmuli into deep snow and rolled him around in it. The fire consuming him died. I crouched down beside him and pulled him into my arms for an embrace. His clothes were in tatters, but he seemed unhurt. Tears filled our eyes.

Before I knew what was happening, my arms were empty again. Someone had snatched Shmuli right out of them. Kaspar stood above us, holding my brother by the scruff of his neck in one hand and an unsheathed knife in the other. Shmuli's face was a mask of terror.

"You lying ass," the giant man sneered. "Did you imagine, even for a moment, that you could get the best of Kaspar?"

I stopped myself from replying, for I could see Elena tiptoeing toward Kaspar behind his back. She was brandishing a large tree branch. When she got close enough, she swung it with all her might against his temple. The redheaded devil fell to the ground with a thud.

"You!" he groaned, staring at Elena. "I know you!" Then his eyes closed and he went still.

"Forgive me, Natan, for failing to listen to you," Elena pleaded.

"I've never been happier to see anyone," I said. I gathered a stunned Shmuli into my arms once more. "Now let's run as fast as we can."

We headed toward a copse of trees at the edge of the field. I didn't know where they led, but I didn't care. All that mattered was that nobody was following us. The woods were so dense that daylight was an unknown visitor.

"Faster! Faster!" I cried as we penetrated the darkness.

CHAPTER 23

We trudged through the thick vegetation, the branches scraping our faces and the snow crunching under our feet. I led the way with Shmuli behind me and Elena at the rear. It was so dark that we could barely see the trees ahead of us. Our teeth were chattering in the cold winter morn.

As we made our way through the darkness, my mind teemed with memories I wanted to forget. The woods disappeared and I was back in the cemetery. I saw flames and heard screams and smelled a stench too horrible to contemplate. Mama was being consumed by fire; Papa, his beard alight, was tossing my brother into my arms. I wept, I screamed, I cursed, I shook my fist at the sky, but the sight of Shmuli's frightened little face silenced my anguish.

I picked him up and held him so close that our tears mingled.

"I want my mama. I want my papa," he wept.

"Mama and Papa are here"—I pointed to his heart—"and here," I added, pointing to my own. "We can't see them, but we can feel them always. They're a part of us now. Never forget that."

He put his head on my shoulder and began to suck his thumb. "Where are we going? When are we going to be there?"

"We're going somewhere nice and we'll be there soon."

Elena plucked my sleeve. "Natan, listen!"

There was smoke in the air and I heard the murmur of voices. I put Shmuli down. He began to cry again.

I parted the branches and we found ourselves at the edge of an encampment. Two caravans stood at the side of the clearing, with several horses tied to a pole beside them. A dozen Gypsy women in bright skirts and colorful headscarves sat around a campfire on low stools. The smell of the stew in their cauldron made my mouth water. Another woman was bent over her lap, mending a shirt by the light of the flames. A young woman was cuddling an infant as she nursed him. There were also several men around the fire. Children were everywhere—laughing, chatting, playing tag or absorbed in a serious game of marbles. When we appeared, silence fell over the camp.

A bowlegged older man with a droopy mustache stepped forward.

"Who are you?" he asked gruffly, in the manner of a lord speaking to his serfs.

Four younger men hauled themselves up from their seats and surrounded him. My heart began to beat faster when I noted that all of them had knives.

"Who are you?" the older man repeated.

"We're fugitives, trying to save the life of this child." I pointed at Shmuli, who was still bawling.

"What do you want from us?"

The armed young men stepped closer.

"Leave them alone!" a shrill voice cried suddenly. "These are the people who saved me from the torment of those awful urchins."

The men parted to let through an old woman. We recognized her instantly as the Gypsy mother we came upon being mocked and pelted by stones. Elena rushed over to her, clasped her hands and fell to her knees.

"Please help us, Nadya! Please, I beg of you. You told us that we could come to you whenever we needed help. That time has arrived!"

"Don't kneel in front of me, mistress," Nadya implored.

The old woman helped my beloved off the ground. Between sobs and hiccups, Elena told the Gypsies our tale.

"So you see," she concluded, "we have nowhere else to go, but we must keep Shmuli safe somehow."

Nadya and the older man had listened to her carefully. When Elena was finished speaking, Nadya drew the man aside. She was talking to him with great intensity, but he kept on shaking his head.

"He won't listen to her," Elena whispered in agony.

Just then, a ragged child came close and pulled on Shmuli's arm, pointing toward the game of marbles two boys were playing on the icy ground. Shmuli stopped crying and clung to me.

"You may go and play with him," I said.

With his thumb in his mouth, Shmuli followed the child hesitantly.

One of the younger women by the fire stood up and declared, "The boy needs warmer clothes." She wrapped the blanket she had been sitting on around Shmuli's shoulders, but he was already so absorbed in his game that he didn't even notice.

I kept my eyes on Nadya and the older man. My heart lifted when he finally threw his arms into the air and nodded. Nadya broke out in a toothless grin and led him back to us.

"This is Roman, my husband and our leader. He has agreed to help you," she said.

"Only a foolish man withstands the persuasion of a determined wife," Roman chuckled. "You can count on us. We'll hide and care for your little brother."

Suddenly, we heard the faint noise of twigs being broken in the distance and snow being trampled in the woods beyond.

"Hush!" Roman said, lifting his hand in warning. The entire camp fell quiet. "Someone's coming."

"You must hide," Nadya said.

She scooped Shmuli up from the ground and hurried us into one of the caravans.

"Climb in!" she said, pointing to a large bin full of used clothing and rags. She pulled the rags over our heads. "Don't talk and try not to move," she warned before leaving.

As soon as she'd left, Shmuli began to whimper.

"Hush!" I soothed. "If you're good, you'll get a sweetmeat."

Nadya had failed to close the caravan's door, so we could hear everything going on outside. There was the sound of bushes being parted and somebody coughing. I pushed the rags aside and lifted my head cautiously out of the bin. I could see through the door to the scene outside.

Kaspar and the same two who were with him when he'd murdered me were standing in the clearing. The redheaded ogre had a large bandage wrapped around his head. I tried to control the terrible hatred that flooded my heart at the sight of him.

"Gypsies," he cried, "where are the fugitives we seek?"

Roman, who had crouched down by the fire while Nadya hid us, stood up in a lively manner.

"Peace be with you, master," he said. "How can we be of assistance?"

"Don't play the fool, man!" Kaspar snarled. He stepped forward and pulled out his knife.

Roman's bodyguards stood up, their own knives drawn, but they didn't move any closer to Kaspar. After a moment, Roman nodded to them and they sat down again.

"Kind master, please, how can we help you?" Roman said in a voice very different from the proud tones he'd used when addressing us.

"We're looking for a mealymouthed creature and his cheap whore. They have a young Jewish cur with them," Kaspar said. He spat on the ground. "And don't give me your falsehoods. I know what you Gypsies are like. We followed the path of these wretches straight to your camp."

"But dear master, we saw no one," Roman said, wringing his hands. "They must have turned and left by the same path when they saw us."

"Why would they do that?"

Roman smiled slyly. "Some of the good burghers don't trust my people. I don't understand why."

But Kaspar was unconvinced. "If you're so innocent, you won't object to our looking around your camp."

Roman nodded. "Go ahead."

I ducked under the rags again. When I heard someone walk into the caravan, I held Shmuli in a close embrace, willing him to be still. I prayed to God that the intruder wouldn't hear us breathing.

"I don't see anyone here, but let me make sure!" It was Kaspar.

"Good idea," somebody else answered.

Kaspar's voice was so loud that he must have been standing very close to the bin in which we were hiding. Then suddenly, a knife plunged through the rags, barely missing my arm.

"Nobody here," Kaspar said angrily, pulling up his knife. I heard him and his companion walk away. The door of the caravan was slammed shut. We began to breathe again.

After a few more minutes of shouting outside and the pounding of horses' hoofs, somebody came into the caravan again.

"It's me, Nadya. You can come out now. They searched every nook and cranny for you. Finally, they gave up and left."

We pushed the rags aside and she helped us climb out of the bin. Our limbs were cramped and full of pins and needles.

"Stretch your arms and legs, Shmuli," Elena said as she massaged his back.

"I was a good boy. Where is my sweetmeat?" he asked.

"You deserve it," Nadya replied, reaching into the pocket of her apron and pulling one out. "I always keep some sweets in my pocket for the children," she explained.

We all returned to the campfire.

"We can't stay here. It's too dangerous for you," I told Roman. "We can't risk the safety of your people."

The old man scratched his head thoughtfully. "You and your lady are difficult to hide. But one small child"—he grinned—"that's easy. Leave the boy with us. We'll take good care of him."

"We'll hide him in plain sight. No one will notice if there is another Gypsy child," Nadya said. "He'll be safe. I'll make sure that his hair is covered to hide the fact that he isn't one of ours." She ruffled Shmuli's bright locks. "I go to your town square every Thursday morn to earn a few coins. I'll take the boy with me each time. If you want him back, come and get him before the cathedral bells strike four times in the afternoon. That's when I usually return home."

I leaned down to say good-bye to Shmuli. "Behave yourself and do as Nadya and Roman tell you. And remember, you must never tell anybody who you are," I warned. "If anybody asks you, your new name is Samson."

He was so eager to return to his friends that he paid no heed. Nadya and Roman brushed our thanks aside.

"I told you that our people have long memories," Nadya said. "You came to my aid and now it's my turn to help you."

Elena and I set out for home, making our cautious way back through the darkened woods toward Strasbourg.

"We'll stay in Rabbi Weltner's house. Nobody will think of looking for us there."

"What if Kaspar finds us?" Elena asked.

"He won't. Why would he search for us in Judenstrasse? We'll be safe at Rabbi Weltner's."

We were so exhausted by the time we reached the outskirts of town that we could barely walk. Elena was leaning heavily on me as we trudged through the deserted streets. All that changed as we approached the synagogue on Judenstrasse.

"Listen!" Elena said.

We could hear shouting and loud thumps, and there was the unmistakable smell of flames.

"Something's burning," I cried.

We broke into a run. The burning smell became stronger as we turned the corner. We looked toward the synagogue and could see a bonfire raging and a mob of people throwing all kinds of sacred objects into the flames. I drew Elena into the shadows of a building on the other side of the street.

"Look at those thieves!" I cried, my hands balled into fists. "I have to stop them somehow."

Elena pulled me back. "Use your head. There are too many of them, and if they see you, they will kill you."

She was right. All I could do was stand there, trembling in anger. I watched one vandal remove the silver crown of a Torah scroll and then toss the scroll itself into the flames. As a sign of victory, his friend held up two heavy silver candlesticks that he had plundered. A third man ran out of the synagogue brandishing a large *shofar*, the ram's horn we used to welcome the Jewish New Year each fall.

"What you got there?" asked the man with the candlesticks.

"I don't rightly know. Looks like some kind of a horn."

"Why would they keep one of them things in their church?" the first man asked, slurring his words as if drunk.

"I know!" cried the one with the candlesticks. "Them Jews must use that horn to betray us. They signal other Jews outside the city walls with it!"

"Ya, you're probably right," the first man slurred. "They're like fleas, them Jews. When you kill one, ten others take its place. The sooner they're gone from Strasbourg, the better it is for the rest of us."

CHAPTER 24

The moon was in the sky by the time we arrived at Rabbi Weltner's house. Too tired to eat, I stoked the hearth to life and we lay down beside it. Despite my fatigue I tossed and turned, and when I finally did sleep I had another dream:

I'm running through a dark tunnel. The only sound is my own heavy breathing. Suddenly, I see a light far, far away. I force myself to go even faster. Just a few more steps, just a few more steps, I tell myself.

When I finally arrive at the end, Hans is waiting for me with his arms and legs spread, blocking my way.

"I want to go home! I want to go home! Let me go home!" he begs, tears running down his face.

I awoke to the sound of Elena's gentle breathing, but I couldn't fall back to sleep. The tortured face of Hans wouldn't leave my mind. I dressed in my tunic and stoked the fire again, and as I did, my mind wandered to a different fire. I thought of Mama and Papa and wise Rabbi Weltner, forever lost to me. I wept until I had no more tears left.

I forced myself to think about happier times. Then I thought of Elena telling me she loved me while Kaspar and his minions drove us to the cemetery. I gazed on her sleeping form. Her eyes were closed, and she was faintly snoring. She was the most beautiful girl I'd ever seen, inside and out.

I ran my fingers over my own pitted face and patted the softness of my paunch. Regret filled my heart. I wished I looked the way I used to—tall and straight and strong, without blemishes distorting my complexion. But that person belonged in the past. I remembered the thud of the shovelfuls of dirt hitting my casket. The vessel was broken yet its contents remained. Was Elena able to see that?

Just then, her eyes fluttered open. She sat up and stretched her arms wide.

"Sleep well?" I asked.

"Like a babe." She wrapped her blanket around her shoulders. "You lit the fire? It's so nice and warm here." She stood up and reached for the gown she had thrown on the floor the night before. "I'll get dressed and get us something to eat. There is still a bit of bread left. We also have some ale."

"Let us talk before you go."

She sat back down, a look of concern on her face. "Are you worried about Shmuli? Nadya has a big heart. She'll take good care of him."

"I don't doubt that. He'll be fine with her, but we can't leave him for long." I leaned over and took her hand between mine. "I want to talk to you about something else right now, though. Do you remember what you said to me when I was on my way to the cemetery?"

Her cheeks turned pink. She nodded shyly.

"Did you mean it, or were you just being kind?"

"You mean, when I told you that I loved you?" she whispered.

My heart began to hammer. "Yes," I managed to croak.

She took a deep breath. "I didn't want you to think me bold, but I had to tell you how I felt in case I didn't see you again."

I looked deep into her eyes. It felt as if I were peering into her very soul. "Do you mean what you're saying?"

"I do. I love you. I love how brave you are. I love how kind you are. I love that I can always count on you."

She put her head on my shoulder and I was filled with joy. But there was another question I had yet to ask.

"I love you too," I said, kissing her palm.

I didn't miss the slight twitch of her fingers that signaled she wanted to disengage them from my grasp. My question was answered before I'd even asked it. I dropped her hand.

"What's the matter?" She stared at me anxiously.

"You love me, but I don't make your heart sing. Not like before," I said bleakly.

She clutched my hands. "I love you, Hans. Please believe me!"

"You called me Hans."

She clamped a hand over her lips, then whispered urgently, "I love you."

"Elena, I must know the truth. Your feelings are different, aren't they?"

"My heart is filled with love for you," she pleaded.

"But not like before?" I pressed.

She turned her head and gazed away. I wished I knew what she was seeing.

"No," she said finally. "Not like before. I'm sorry."

CHAPTER 25

The rest of the day, both of us behaved as if nothing unusual had happened. We ate our bread, drank our ale and spoke of everything except what we most wanted to speak about. Time passed slowly. After three days, I was pacing like a caged animal, desperate to go outside into the white world beyond the house.

"You're restless," Elena observed.

"I feel like a prisoner."

"Me too." She stared through the window at the gray sky outside. "We have to find some food or we'll starve. A crust of the bread is all that's left."

"Let's go to the town square. There might be some hawkers there."

She shook her head. "There won't be. They have nothing to sell. Food is scarce nowadays."

"Even if we don't find anything, we'll see Shmuli. I already miss him, and Nadya will have him in the square. It's Thursday today."

Her face brightened. "It'll be good to see him."

"We'll have to be careful, though. Kaspar will be looking for us."

We dressed in our warmest clothing, careful to pull our hoods low over our heads. The wind was blowing icy snow into our faces as we trudged along the empty streets. Most of the shops were still shuttered. We passed more houses with red crosses painted on their doors. Bodies were still stacked up like firewood along the side of the road. The snow coated everything, making the world seem white and pure—until I noticed a woman's naked body surrounded by two wild pigs. I dared not look at what they were doing to her and hastened my steps, pulling Elena alongside me.

Finally, we arrived in the town square. It was almost empty except for a few stragglers and the Gypsies. They seemed to be everywhere. Roman was selling roasted chestnuts from a cart, and young Gypsy women were peddling colorful blankets and scarves to the few people in the square. Their children were playing in the snow. Nadya was standing in front of the cathedral, shaking a tambourine. A young boy dressed in rags was beside her, a cup in his hand to catch any

coins thrown to the old woman. It took me a moment
to recognize him beneath the grime over his face. Only
a lock of bright hair peeking from beneath his cap gave
him away. It was Shmuli. He saw me just as I saw him,
and before I could warn him not to acknowledge me,
he flew into my arms.

"Natan! Natan!" he cried. "When can I go home?"

"Hush! We don't want anybody to notice us."

Nadya walked up to us, huffing and puffing in the
snow.

"The boy is an imp. You can't turn your back on him
for a second. Have you come to take him home?" She
patted his face. "I'll miss him, for sure."

"I'll take him instead!" a loud voice announced
behind me.

I spun around to stare into Kaspar's grinning face.
Several guardsmen were standing beside him. He
plucked Shmuli out of my arms and dangled him in the
air by the scruff of his neck.

Elena jumped forward. "Leave him alone!" she
cried, tugging on my brother's arm.

"Ah! At last, my pretty little pigeon." The ogre
grabbed her wrist. "Shame on you! You should have
listened when I told you that nobody outsmarts
Kaspar."

Elena turned as white as the snow glistening at the
ends of her lashes.

I felt powerless and prayed to God to help me save the only people I had left to love in the entire world.

"Let them go!" I said.

Kaspar burst into laughter.

Such fury engulfed me that it made me tremble. "Let them go or you'll regret it!"

"Why? What'll you do to me?" Kaspar taunted.

Without warning, something large and dark knocked against him and he fell to the ground, letting go of Shmuli and Elena at the same time. His henchmen also fell. Everything had happened so quickly that it took me a moment to realize what had occurred. Roman was on the ground, his cart upended and the chestnuts rolling over the icy cobblestones. Both Kaspar and his men had slipped on them.

"I'm sorry, master," Roman said in an obsequious tone, winking at me behind Kaspar's back. "The square is so slippery."

"Run!" I yelled to Elena, pointing away from the rolling chestnuts. "Run that way!"

She picked up her skirts and was on her way. I followed her with Shmuli's hand clutched firmly in mine. I looked back only once. Kaspar had pulled himself off the ground and was in pursuit at the far end of the square.

"Hurry! Hurry!" I cried. We took every lane and street that would lead us back to Rabbi Weltner's house by the most circuitous route possible. When we finally arrived, there were only two people in Judenstrasse. A woman was holding on to a man's arm as they made their way cautiously over the cobblestones. They were too far away for me to see their faces, but it didn't really matter. They weren't Kaspar.

"I don't want to leave you!" Shmuli cried when we settled him by the hearth.

I patted his shoulder. "You're a good boy—strong and brave. You'll do what's expected of you."

"What do you mean, Natan?" Elena asked. "Surely, you'll keep—"

I interrupted her. "Let's talk about this another time. The boy must be hungry."

Elena gave him the last of our bread and he wolfed it down. She and I went to bed hungry.

As before, I tossed and turned, worrying myself sick with thoughts of Kaspar and our lack of food. When I finally did fall asleep, I was once again running through a tunnel toward a light. And once again, Hans blocked my way and begged me to let him come home.

CHAPTER 26

I don't know how many hours had passed when I was woken by the noise of somebody knocking on the front door. I grabbed a knife and hurried to answer it, for I didn't want Elena and Shmuli disturbed. To my surprise, Meyer the moneylender was standing in the doorway, holding a large sack in his hand. I ushered him into the house.

"I'm sorry to disturb you in the middle of the night," he said.

"Come in, come in!" I was so glad to see him that I hugged him. "How did you stay alive? Your house was quarantined, so I knew you must have had the plague."

The old man brushed the snow off his shoulders.

"It's good to see you too, Hans," he said. "We're alive because the good Lord spared us. By the time we had recovered, though, all our friends and relatives were burned." He wiped away the tears that had pooled in his eyes. "We just found out that you were hiding at the house of Rabbi Weltner of blessed memory," he continued. "My wife and I were in the town square this afternoon, looking for food. We were helping ourselves to the meat of a fallen goat when we noticed you. It would have been hard not to with all the screaming and yelling Kaspar was doing. We saw everything that happened, and afterward—forgive me—we followed you. You didn't notice us because we were so far behind, but we saw you duck into the rabbi's house. May God bless you for saving Shmuli!" He held his bloody sack out toward me. "I brought you some of the goat meat. The boy has to eat. So do you, and the girl too. There is enough here for all of you."

"Thank you. We were getting desperate for food."

He sighed. "These are tough times, especially for Jews like us and little Shmuli. Did you hear what happened in the synagogue?"

"We saw it being looted. I felt so powerless at being unable to stop the thieves."

"Don't blame yourself, Hans. There were so many of them." He looked at me sadly. "Anyway, I came to say good-bye. We must leave our beloved Strasbourg. It doesn't matter that I was born here—as was my father and his father before him, as long back as anybody can remember. Now we must leave in the middle of the night, like thieves, never to return." He touched his heart. "It's hard."

"Where will you go?"

"My cousin lives in a small hamlet on the other side of the mountains. It's a peaceful place, and we're too old for excitement." He wiped his eyes. "It'll be a good life—a life we can live with our heads held high."

Suddenly, I realized what I had to do. "Take Shmuli with you!" I blurted. "Please take my brother with you."

"Your *brother*? What are you saying, Hans?"

I had no choice but to tell him everything. I told him that I was an *ibbur*, and that I had taken possession of Hans's body. I told him that with his dying breath, my father had pleaded with me to help my brother. Tears ran freely down my cheeks. "Please," I begged, "you must believe me!"

Amazement, disbelief and wonder were at war on his face until finally he nodded. "I *do* believe you. You have told me things that only Natan could know." He grabbed my arm and pulled me closer, peering into my eyes as if he could see into my very soul. "Yes," he said after a moment. "You *are* Natan. I can see it with my own tired eyes. During my studies with Rabbi Weltner, I read about such things, but to come face to face with an *ibbur* . . ." He gave me a frightened look.

"Please don't be afraid of me. I'm a failure. The Almighty gave me the opportunity to save my people, but I couldn't do it. I couldn't fulfill the mission God set for me." I hung my head, for I was too ashamed meet his eyes. "Our people were burned."

"But you did fulfill your mission," Meyer whispered vehemently.

I hid my face in my hands. "Don't mock me, please. I can't bear it."

"Natan, have you forgotten what our sages said?"

"What do you mean?"

"The Talmud says, 'Whoever saves a life, it is considered as if he saved the world.' You saved your brother."

As I stared at him, trying to take it all in, joy and sadness flooded my being. I looked at Elena, unaware in her sleep. I knew that I had to break her heart. But first, there was something else I had to do.

I turned back to old Meyer. "Please take my brother with you," I repeated.

"Why do you want Shmuli to go with us?"

"Because you are of our people and you are a kind man. Because with you, he'll be able to live the life he was meant to live." I looked again at Elena, still peacefully asleep. "Because I must leave soon."

He grasped my hands. "All right, my friend. I promise that we will take good care of your brother. He will be the son we prayed for and never had—until now."

—#—

After Meyer had gone, I sat down by the hearth, trying to decide how to tell Shmuli that he would soon be leaving me. As I watched him sleeping by the hearth, so pure and innocent, he suddenly began to cry out, "Mama, Papa, where are you? Where are you?"

I touched him lightly on the shoulder.

He sat up, rubbing his eyes. "I had such a bad dream," he said. "Mama and Papa were in the fire." He began to weep. "I want Mama!"

"Shh! Elena is sleeping." I drew him close. "Do you remember when I told you that we would always carry Mama and Papa in our hearts?"

He nodded and cuddled closer to me.

"They want you to be a good boy. I know that for sure."

He began to sob again. "I miss them so much!"

Elena opened her eyes and sat up, wrapping her blanket around her shoulders. "What's the matter?"

"I have to tell Shmuli a secret."

My brother stopped crying and his thumb found its way into his mouth. "What secret?"

I took a deep breath. "Our parents of blessed memory want Meyer and Miriam, his wife, to take care of you."

"But I don't want—"

I wouldn't let him finish. "Mama and Papa still love you. They will always love you. That's why they want you to go away with Meyer and Miriam and be their little boy. A little boy like you needs parents."

"I don't want to go away with them. I want to stay here with you!" he said fiercely.

"Meyer and Miriam are good people. They'll give you a good home—a Jewish home, like Mama and Papa wanted for you."

"I don't care!" Shmuli sobbed. "I want to be with you."

"May I speak to you, Natan?" Elena asked, drawing me to the far side of the room. She was pale, with her lips pinched together. "Shmuli is right," she said under her breath. "You're his brother. You should be together. Why are you sending him away?"

I couldn't tell her the truth—not yet.

"My parents would want this for him," I said simply.

She turned her head away. "I'd make a good mother," she whispered.

"And someday you will. But you must trust me. I'm doing the right thing sending Shmuli away with Meyer and his wife."

She gave me an injured look. "Is it because I'm not of your faith?"

I couldn't help laughing. "Oh, Elena, I wish that were our only problem."

Just then, we heard banging outside.

"They're here," Elena said, and she went to open the door.

Shmuli hid his head in my chest and wrapped his arms around my waist. He wouldn't look at Meyer and Miriam.

"Natan will come and see you all the time, won't you, Natan?" Miriam said reassuringly as she patted his back.

I noticed that she gave me a curious look when she called me by my name.

"I'll come when I can." I didn't want to lie.

Meyer crouched down beside Shmuli. "Miriam and I prayed for a long time for a little boy just like you," he said quietly. "Your mama and papa would want us to care for you, just as your brother says."

The old man held out his hand, and after a tense moment, Shmuli took it. By the time they left, he was listening with rapt attention to Miriam's tale about a mule at her cousin's house.

"Nobody feeds him, washes him or exercises him," she exclaimed. "He is waiting for you to come and take care of him. Will you do it?"

Shmuli nodded solemnly. When they left, he didn't even look back.

CHAPTER 27

Elena and I stared at each other unhappily when the door closed behind them.

"Why did you send him away?" she cried.

"I did the right thing, Elena. You must accept that."

She stared at the rosy sky through the window for a long time, then finally said. "Yes, you're right. He'll be happy with Meyer and his wife, but I'll miss him."

"So will I."

She met my gaze. "What's the matter? You seem preoccupied. Is there something more you're keeping from me?"

I busied myself with throwing a log on the hearth and pretended not to hear her question.

I wondered if she realized how dear she was to me? How a movement of her hands, a smile on her lips, a turn of her cheek spoke to me? But this wasn't the time to tell her.

"Let's go for a walk. It'll clear my head," I said.

"But Kaspar—"

"Let's forget about him for once."

She looked puzzled but draped her cloak around her shoulders without any more questions and we set out. The rays of the rising sun turned the world into a pink wonderland. It was the most beautiful sight I'd ever seen, so fresh and full of promise.

We headed toward the River Ill. As we walked along the bank, I noticed that the ice over the water was beginning to melt. A few green leaves were thrusting their heads out of the snow along our path. Spring was in the air. I parted the bulrushes and we sat down on the same boulder we had occupied on the day of the town fair. I took her into my arms. The scent of her made the blood pound in my veins. She rested her head on my shoulders. I felt more alive than ever before. Suddenly, I knew what I had to say.

"I must leave you now, my love. My work is done. I will love you to eternity. Good-bye."

I pulled her closer until there was nothing else except our two bodies pressed together and our two hearts beating as one. I kissed her. The next moment, the world became brighter than the sun. Fire ran through my body and I had to let her go. My arms felt empty. I was in a tunnel, running toward a light so bright that I had to close my eyes. When I opened them again, I was home.

ELENA'S STORY

CHAPTER 28

It broke my heart to allow Shmuli to leave, but it wasn't up to me to decide his fate. Natan was his brother, and when I saw the dear little boy with Meyer and his wife, I had to confess that he'd made the right decision. This was what his parents would have wanted for Shmuli.

But I sensed that Natan was holding something back from me. It made me feel embarrassed when he looked at me as if I were the most precious object he had ever beheld. It was the same way I used to look at him . . . before.

We went to the riverbank, and everything was so crisp and new. Then he pulled me close and kissed me, and it all fell into place. All that mattered was for us to be together. The memory of the curly-haired boy who had captured my heart became just that—a memory. I turned toward him to confess my love, but before I could utter a single word, there was an unbearable brightness and my arms were empty.

Suddenly, it was Hans who was sitting next to me on the boulder. When I gazed into his eyes, I knew with absolute certainty that I was looking at my father's journeyman. My Natan was gone and he had left me behind.

"I'm tired," Hans yawned, running his fingers through his limp hair. "My head aches."

"I hope that you're not sickening with the Great Pestilence."

"The plague is in Strasbourg?" His voice was full of fear.

I swallowed hard. "Yes, my papa is gone."

He grasped my fingers. "He is?! But you must miss him so much!" He blinked and I saw that there were tears glistening in his eyes. "I'll miss him too. He was a fair master and a good man." His words brought back memories of Natan. "I'll do anything I can to help you, Elena. Just tell me what you need."

I nodded. "Thank you."

He leaned closer. "It's odd," he said, scratching his head. "I feel as if I've been on a long journey, yet I have no memories of what I've seen." He stood up. "I know it's nonsense. I must have been here with you the whole time?"

"Yes, you were."

He gave a sigh of relief and extended his hand to pull me up. "Just as I thought," he said. "Let's go home."

———#———

We returned to my father's house. As the days melted into nights, I sat by the hearth, waiting for the world to end as the plague raged outside my door. And yet I barely noticed the death surrounding me, for my mind was full of him. How I wished to tell him that he made the blood pound in my veins. How I wished to tell him that I could barely remember how he looked when we first met. How I wished to tell him that when I thought of his marked face and lank hair, my heart sang for him. Just like before.

EPILOGUE

The world did not end. Time passed and the Great Pestilence left Strasbourg. Then it came back again and again, until finally it was gone for a long, long time. Those of us who survived began to rebuild our lives. I opened Papa's shop with the help of Hans. He kept on asking me to marry him, but I always refused. It wouldn't have been fair to him, not with my heart given to another.

The plague did not discriminate. It visited everyone, both the good and the wicked. Vera had joined the angels with her sister. Even Kaspar had to face his maker before he found me.

After a while, we began to live normal lives. Sometimes, late at night, I felt that my beloved was lying by my side. But when I stretched out my arm toward him, there was no one there. I never saw Natan again, except in my dreams.

AUTHOR'S NOTE

Another Me is a work of fiction, but it's based on a true historical event. During the Middle Ages, the bubonic plague raged through Europe, killing half the population. In 1349, Jews living in the Free Imperial City of Strasbourg were accused of poisoning the town wells to cause an outbreak of this plague, which is also known as the Black Death or the Great Pestilence. This was an obvious lie, but many citizens believed it and others seized on it as an excuse to do harm.

On February 14, 1349, the two thousand Jewish inhabitants of Strasbourg were led to their deaths in the Jewish cemetery by Peter Schwarber, the city's former Ammeister. They were burned alive on large wooden platforms that had been erected over the graves, just as depicted in the novel. But despite this supposed precaution, the plague still arrived in Strasbourg, where it took a terrible toll. Historical documents vary about the date the disease first appeared in the city.

Both Jews and Christians fell victim to the plague, although it is true that there were far fewer Jewish deaths. We know now that the plague was spread by fleas hosting on infected rats. When the rats died, the fleas looked for new hosts, including people. Observant Jews—who must wash their hands upon arising, before eating bread and before prayer—lived under more sanitary conditions that were less favorable to the spread of this horrendous disease.

As portrayed in the novel, the synagogue of Strasbourg was pillaged. Among other items, the looters found a ram's horn, or *shofar*, used in synagogue services such as the High Holidays in the fall. The people of Strasbourg erroneously believed that the Jews intended to betray the city by signaling their allies outside the town walls. All remaining Jews were banished from Strasbourg.

The city fathers ordered two copies of this ram's horn to be cast in bronze. One of them, the Grusselhorn, was sounded every evening at eight o'clock to warn any Jews still inside the walls of Strasbourg to leave the city. The second horn was sounded at midnight to remind people of the supposed Jewish plot that was averted on February 14, 1349. By 1368, however, some Jews had returned to Strasbourg. More and more went back to their city, until another banishment edict was issued in 1388.

Except for Peter Schwarber, all the characters in my novel are figments of my imagination. Was there really an *ibbur* called Natan who lived in Strasbourg during these terrible times and loved a girl called Elena? That is for you to decide.

ACKNOWLEDGMENTS

I would like to thank my family for their support and belief in me. As always, my husband, Nathan, was my first reader and editor, closely followed by my daughter, Marni. Their input was invaluable to me.

Several people were generous with their time and knowledge. They include Millie Acheson, Rabbi Avraham Altein, Rabbi Alan Green and Gisela Persaud. My editors, Sue Tate and Janice Weaver, never led me wrong.

The ballad "Under the Linden," quoted in chapter 13, was written by Walther von der Vogelweide (ca. 1170–ca. 1230), perhaps the most famous German medieval poet. In chapter 19, I quote from the Catholic prayer for the dead. The rest of the poetry and songs in the book are my own.

Finally, I would like to acknowledge the support of the Canada Council for the Arts during the writing of this book.

 Canada Council   Conseil des arts
for the Arts   du Canada

GLOSSARY

Ammeister: An important guild member and head of the city council.

bloodletting: The removal of a sick person's blood, using leeches or cutting, to cure or prevent illness.

cholent: A Jewish dish of vegetables and meat, usually eaten for lunch on the Sabbath.

guild: A group of tradesmen or artisans uniting to provide mutual protection and to advance their business interests. The guild system was a key part of the economy and society of Europe between the eleventh and sixteenth centuries.

Hashem: A Hebrew word for God.

journeyman: The middle of the three ranks (apprentice, journeyman and master) in the guild system. A journeyman had completed his apprenticeship and was able to work for a master in exchange for wages. He could become a master himself once he had proved his competence in his trade.

master: The highest rank in the guild system. The master was an established tradesman who ran his own shop and thus enjoyed greater wealth and a higher social status.

miasma: Corrupt, or "bad," air. Physicians in the Middle Ages believed that the plague introduced bad air into the body through the lungs or pores in the skin. This miasma then poisoned the body and caused sickness. People feared breathing in the bad air of plague victims. In the most dreaded scenario, the miasma from a dying person's eyes entered a healthy person's eyes resulting in immediate death.

pallet: A simple or makeshift bed.

pottage: A hearty soup or stew.

poultice: A soft mixture of herbs or other medicinal plants spread on a cloth and placed on the skin to heal a sore or reduce pain.

prior: A high-ranking member of a religious order.

privy: A toilet found in a small shed out back of a house.

Shabbos: The Jewish Sabbath, a day of rest and religious observance. It begins with sunset on Friday night and ends with nightfall on Saturday. Traditionally, the Shabbos is welcomed with a synagogue service followed by a festive meal in the home.

shofar: A ram's-horn trumpet used during certain Jewish religious services.

Talmud: A collection of ancient rabbinic writings in Judaism, the most significant text for interpreting the Torah.

Torah: The five books of Moses found in the Hebrew Bible. Also called the Pentateuch. In synagogue, the Torah is read from a scroll.

treacle: A medicinal compound used to treat all manner of illnesses in the Middle Ages.